Practical Obsession

PRACTICAL OBSESSION

The
UNAUTHORIZED
AUTOBIOGRAPHY
of a
MAD MYSTIC

N. Nosirrah

Illustrations by A. Nosirrah and B. Nosirrah

SENTIENT PUBLICATIONS

SENTIENT PUBLICATIONS

A Limited Liability Company
1113 Spruce Street
Boulder, CO 80302
www.sentientpublications.com

PUBLISHER'S PREFACE

For the many scholarly researchers into the life of N. Nosirrah, we have very little verified information on the facts of this renowned mystic's history. As you will see as you read the pages of Nosirrah's autobiography, his sense of time, geography and even location in his body or in the body of someone else is an ever mutating expression of his transcendental vision. We have tried to piece together some of the fragments of his life in the following paragraphs to give the general reader, and not just the academics who seem so fascinated by this amazing man, a sense of Nosirrah's life.

There are references to Nosirrah's birth in *God Is an Atheist* that would place the blessed event in the year 1923 or 1924 in Berlin, Germany or possibly Paris, France. However, it is not clear from his writing whether this is accurate or a passing reverie on the part of Nosirrah, who suggests that he may be the bastard son of Alice B. Toklas and Franz Kafka. It is clear from historic research that Toklas and Kafka were both in Berlin in 1923, and that Toklas was at the end of her childbearing years, however there is no clear record of Toklas and Gertrude Stein raising a child as indicated in this book. That lack of historic reference to a child does not in and of itself disprove Nosirrah's childhood, as he clearly suggests that Toklas and Stein hid and denied his existence as a pathway to preserving their relationship to each other in the face of the carnal indiscretions between Toklas and Kafka that may have begat Nosirrah. Whether this secret childhood is a historic fact lost to any who have chronicled the lives of Stein and Toklas or a metaphor for Nosirrah's profound sense of no-self is something that historians and scholars will no doubt debate for many years to come.

Nosirrah goes into great detail about his life in this autobiographical work, however there is no direct reference to his date of birth. He does indicate that he died shortly after birth, which is assumed to be either a near death experience or a clinical death with an extraordinary recovery, and not simply a metaphor, as this event seems to have fundamentally altered his state of consciousness. We can summarize by saying that he has lived in an altered state throughout his life and largely recounts his attempts to integrate that state of being, to communicate it, and to find his way to others who might share that energetic state. Nosirrah reveals himself to be a true master of mind and consciousness, a traveler through the inner and outer worlds undaunted by any obstacle, and it is for this reason that we find his work to be of such value.

In his book *Chronic Eros,* which was originally a collection of chapters removed from *Practical Obsession* in an attempt by Nosirrah's editor to protect his image as a spiritual master, Nosirrah portrays a world of raucous love, fantastical romance and Eros so convoluted and absent of normal sensitivity and social perception that the reader is left wondering whether he ever really had a relationship with anyone, other than perhaps his muse and the bane of his existence, Lydia, whose full name is thought to be Lydia Smith, or possibly Lydia Smythe (this may be her maiden name), age unknown, although it's likely that she was younger than Nosirrah, who has made clear in all his writings that his interests lie with younger women. It is thought that his editor stimulated Nosirrah's greatest literary works, but may have also been the co-creator of them, perhaps to a larger degree then Nosirrah liked. There are some who suggest that Nosirrah was actually only semi-literate and Lydia was not just his beloved but also his ghostwriter. Accounts of their tumultuous relationship suggest a romantic and possibly carnal relationship, and further indicate that it broke down in anger over another woman. Lydia apparently would never see or speak to Nosirrah again, but would continue to "edit" his work.

In *Chronic Eros*, Nosirrah did claim to have mastered the esoteric inner essence of the *Kama Sutra,* particularly the full lotus mounted butterfly position, and claimed to still have scars to prove it.

Nosirrah seems to have been simultaneously devastated and liberated by the loss of Lydia, producing his most difficult and obscure work, *Nothing from Nothing,* in the ensuing melancholy over the loss of his muse. As he recounts in *God Is an Atheist,* Nosirrah tried to suppress the publication of

Nothing from Nothing, but was apparently too late, as Lydia already had the manuscript. It is clear from the events surrounding this book and its content that there was a second breakdown of Nosirrah's altered mind state, one that he may not have recovered from and which is in evidence in the text of *God Is an Atheist* as well as passages from his doomsday novel, *2013: How to Profit from the Prophets in the Coming End of the World.* This shift seemed to occur when he was a young man, already renowned as a spiritual teacher, when he walked away from his followers, enticed by yet another woman, with whom he sired two sons, known only as A. and B. Nosirrah. Although we know that A. Nosirrah illustrated some of Nosirrah's books, no person has ever come forward admitting to being the offspring of N. Nosirrah.

Nosirrah mentions an E. Amlod in unpublished notes, and this individual is likely to have been an adopted daughter met high in the Himalayan Mountains during Nosirrah's attempt to circle Mt. Kailash, a trip not documented other than with the fact that he was rescued by Amlod, a Tibetan nomad who strapped him to a yak in a semi-conscious state (Nosirrah that is) and delivered him to a doctor in Darchen, Tibet. Amlod had come across Nosirrah attempting to circumambulate himself, having conflated himself with Shiva in a fit of ecstatic mysticism. He had been at it for weeks with little progress. Mt. Kailash, as you may know, is thought of by the Hindus as the seat of Shiva, some would even say it is the embodiment of Shiva. Once removed from the mountain, Nosirrah made a quick recovery and, in gratitude, Nosirrah adopted Amlod, although it is not clear whether this was a legal act or an act of Nosirrah's imagination. Amlod was brought to the West, where she went on to become an artist of some renown, although producing her work under a pseudonym.

Nosirrah fashioned his parenting style after a François Truffaut film he stumbled upon in 1970, which he took to be a documentary on child raising (apparently *The Wild Child*), and seemed pleased that A. and B. could neither read nor write, ate on the ground without the use of their hands, and walked for the most part on all fours.

Nosirrah apparently has some kind of following, although we have never met anyone who has directly met Nosirrah. What is collected here is largely anecdotal and hearsay. Nosirrah himself has written: "Those who understand these writings have no need to meet me, those who do not understand have no reason to meet me, and those who need to meet me have no need to read my writings."

It is not clear whether Nosirrah is alive or not. There is no record of his death, just as there is no clear record of his life. He himself stated very unmistakably that he is not. We do not know the extent of his writings, only what we have found by long searching and many adventures with collectors of rare books.

Few lives have been as fascinating as the life of Nosirrah, or could point so directly to the essential truths of our existence, and more importantly, perhaps, to our non-existence.

If you have any further information on the life of Nosirrah or his work, please let us know so that we can incorporate it into future editions of this autobiography.

I pen this at the behest of those who have traveled with me over not just the dusty miles I have trod, but the seemingly endless years of a life that is more than just odd. Yes, far more than odd, rather a life that is an anomaly of such gargantuan proportion and of such rare defect that it is statistically impossible to have occurred. Yet this very book is proof that the life I will describe did occur. Or is it that it was imagined to have occurred, a dream, an illusion, a story by the self about the self, a self which does not exist, a Nosirrah that does not exist? It is really the same, isn't it — the life and the dream — after all, I am a narcoleptic with hyperthymestic syndrome, I can remember every detail of this life but I am asleep when I remember. This is not so important, although I am told it is unusual, but what is both important and much more than unusual for a narcoleptic hyperthymestic such as I is that I can forget the entirety of my life and be totally awake. Sleeping is a dream, remembering is sleeping, so to be awake is to forget and to forget is to remember who I am not and the life that I never lived.

I refer here to my life, and the oddity is that it is at all, and further, strangely, that it is not a life that will leave any trace that there has been a life at all. Perhaps, rather, one would say it is a blur, or a wave, a movement of some subtle nature, but certainly not a biographical event, historically placed, documented by the detritus of modern day existence, bills paid and unpaid, and photographs of times and places, and possessions made with plastic, glass and chrome. Yet, I am writing this unauthorized autobiography, having not given myself permission to write it, and with no desire to cooperate with such an intrusive book and yet compelled to write it all the same, as accurate a story of the unfolding of Nosirrah as there could ever hope to be. Clearly, it is the fiction of memory, the myth of the self, that there is a biography of a someone when surely we have seen by now that there is indeed life but there is not division of that life called me other than in the imagination, an imagination arising only out of the division, the division arising out of the wholeness and therefore not two at all, just the illusion of two, the imagining of wholeness and the memory of two.

I write this, as I have just said, not for the general public, for they would have no idea of what is being expressed in these pages. The casual reader would not proceed further, putting this work aside for another time, and that other time of course not coming since there are so many other more stimulating activities than to read the nonsensical ravings of a maniacal philosopher who has himself never even read

Heidegger, an enlightened dervish who has never adhered to any religion, a mystic who has transcended the fundamental need to transcend and who accepts his own contradiction, for contradiction is the fodder for philosophy, and Nosirrah lives from the energy of contradiction, or as Heidegger once wrote in his amazing body of work, "making itself intelligible is suicide for philosophy."

No casual reader would have an interest in such apparent drivel. Thankfully.

No, I write this for those who have gone with me from the expansive, unlimited cosmic consciousness, the godhead beyond reality itself, descending through state and form, quality and qualia into the very molten center, the core of lavaic energy.

(And let me be clear that by lavaic I refer to the fiery quality of a volcano, not the well-endowed Martin Lavaic, whom you will remember best from his stand-out performance in the classic film *European Farmhands*, known not for its dialogue, for the words of the film are few, but for the deeds depicted in the film, the profound interactions of the stud farmhands who chop wood, carry water and then roll in the hay with each other unfettered by clothing or the necessity of women, now two, now three, now more, all filmed in that arty, grainy way that tells you this is a film of great substance as well as being anatomically expository. Martin was truly lavaic, as was our relationship, by which I mean a relationship with him that was more than just the 1,143 times I have viewed the phallic follies of *European Farmhands*, a relationship I have never before revealed except once in a glancing reference in my scintillating, banned-in-much-of-the-world-for-good-reason tome, *Chronic Eros*. I cannot be caught up in my memories of Laviac, or I will catch fire even as I write. Martin, wherever you are, we will always have Prague.)

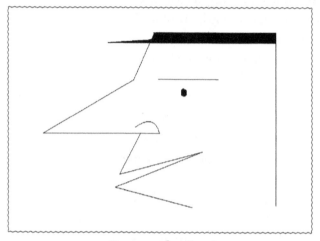

European farmhand

I digress, but molten energy of the third chakra is after all a derivative of the fundamental energy that I allude to above, before the distracting parenthetical comments.

I write for those who have come to me as students, who know that while they will never understand, they must continue to learn, with graduation unattainable and with a teacher who is impossible to please and just as impossible to disappoint. While many have called me a teacher, just as many have called me a madman, only a few have called me what I am: vast nothingness enfolded in the apparition of form, a mirror reflecting the mirror image of itself, a holographic fractal in ten dimensions and three time zones. I don't need to write a coherent sentence because I live in absolute freedom and do not care a whit if you read any more, except if you do read further, and then I care more than anything in the world. If you are not currently my student, then I must break the news to you that it is too late to become one, as I am taking no more students. I have all the students I can possibly handle. The other important point is that I have no students because I am not a teacher. So, not only is it too late, but even if it were not too late, no positions are available. Exceptions will be made for those with large trust funds or young, beautiful women, send pictures and/or copies of your asset accounts to me care of the publisher. I might consider you if it doesn't involve a question about a personal problem, family issues, money issues, health issues, or a philosophical issue that is actually the avoidance of any of the aforementioned personal problems. If you are looking for a sublime experience, an interesting encounter, a mate, a story to tell your friends, or to chalk up one more teacher in your list of teachers you have met, it would probably be better to look elsewhere. Try a Google search on the phrase "spiritual gurus looking for followers" or check Craigslist under "Enlightened Ones seeking Students." What I teach is for everyone and anyone, it is free, it is simple, it doesn't require a teacher or student and so it is available to only the few who don't want the packaging, who don't even want the shiny object within the package, but will settle only for the space that is both inside and outside the package, the shiny object, and students themselves.

Have I digressed from the tale of my life? So I have, let me return, abruptly leaving the subject of the last paragraph and jumping without any connection whatsoever to the next. It seems an inexplicable writing technique until one realizes the deep symbolism of the disconnection of the birth of Nosirrah from anything before it. This birth was a priori, nothing informed it, nothing created it and there was not an experience of it other than Kant rolling over in his grave in Kaliningrad. You didn't know that one of Germany's great philosophers is buried in Russia? That is because he wasn't buried in Russia, he was buried in Germany. World War II changed many boundaries and what was Königsberg, Germany became Kaliningrad, Russia.

I will tell my story as if I had been born, as if I have lived and as if I write these words. You will know that I never was born, that I never lived and another writes these words as if he is Nosirrah, this other is one so vast that there is none other than the other. This is a paradox, but one I have come to accept, I am one and I am none, I write and I don't write, it is my story and it is my truth.

My story is an illustration of the potential of a life and a cautionary tale for those few who will tread the path of inquiry. It may read like a slightly pornographic literary thriller of epic proportions, mythic in its message and dramatic in its unfolding, but I can assure you that everything recounted here is the absolute truth.

Do you question that it is the absolute truth? I can hear your humanist whining, your statements of contradiction, and you shout: "There are no absolute truths!" You are absolutely correct. Get it? Now that you have encased your objections in paradox, let us continue with absolute truth.

I will tell you the absolute truth about my life. If it is absolute truth then it will be universal and applicable in all times, all places, all conditions and all states of consciousness.

Let me give you a clear example of absolute truth: God exists if I am not wrong in my belief in Him.

That wasn't difficult at all and I think we can agree to the truth of that statement and we can challenge anyone, anywhere to refute its truth. This truth is universal and will remain true under all conditions in all times.

So, in this work we will be dealing in absolute truths and you can entirely rely on these throughout.

Have you ever been aware that you are unconscious? I don't mean that you have deduced this condition or been told that you were unconscious, but have you had the direct conscious experience that you were not conscious? I think not, therefore we can say that consciousness is continuous, can we not? It is absolutely true that you cannot be conscious of being unconscious, and therefore you can be conscious only of being conscious, and therefore, consciousness is continuous.

Why is the realization of continuous consciousness important? Two reasons.

First reason: you can now declare yourself enlightened, since continuous consciousness is the goal of enlightenment-seeking spirituality. You did it; you are illuminated, good job! But you need certification and lineage and that certification is available through my company – Enlightenment,

Next Customer!, LLC – for just $99.95, which includes a listing on Sarlo's Guru Rating Service, a wall plaque signed by me allowing you to teach in the name of Nosirrah or anyone else since Nosirrah is one with all beings so if you would rather be authorized by Buddha, Britney Spears or Babe Ruth just fill in the space provided. You will also get a laminated, wallet sized card that you can show as ID when being arrested, at the urgent care clinic when they ask for your insurance card, or if you happen to be traveling in Arizona and are not Caucasian and don't wish to be immediately deported – society has great respect for enlightened beings and we have found this card to be superior to a library card in these situations and just slightly less effective than running away really fast. Plus, you will receive 500 business cards proclaiming you an enlightened being, which is immensely helpful in networking for a job if the unemployment checks are about to run out or if you are speed dating or just want to show your card to your mother when she complains that you are still living at home on your fiftieth birthday. Place the plaque on your wall in your home office, next to your GED and the third place finish in Adult Kickball you won last year and you are good to go: start advising the huddled masses of the unenlightened, confused or just simply bored on how to live the life of truth. Some enlightenment organizations charge thousands of dollars, make you sign over your trust fund or make you do tedious practices like meditation or listening to the senior enlightened leader people droning on about your shortcomings and, let's face it, none of these organizations are going to declare you enlightened in the end anyway. Enlightenment Next Customer!, LLC is the number one enlightenment certification company in the world. And, if you order today, you will get, absolutely free, the exciting companion manual *How to Answer Spiritual Questions with Profound Answers that Will Keep Them Coming in the Door.* This book, valued at $19.95, is yours absolutely free and includes complete instructions on discoursing on crowd pleasers like "Why the Seeker Isn't Trying Hard Enough," "If You Do What I Say for the Next 20 Years You Get to Tell Other People What to Do, But Only If I Say You Can," and the all-time favorite, "If You Question Me, That's Ego, If You Agree with Me, That's Clarity," plus the bonus chapter, "I Have The Microphone and You Don't, So I Can Humiliate You and Make It Seem Like I Am Doing You a Big Favor." You can get all of this free, but you must order now. Call today.

But we were discussing continuous consciousness, and the second reason continuous consciousness is critical is as a literary bridge to the beginning of my life, and hence the beginning of this book, which is, after all, an autobiography, and if I don't get to the story of my life pretty soon it will result in this book not being published. In that case these words would not be entering into your brain, altering that brain fundamentally in the realization of the absolute truth that enlightenment is simply an idea, not a special state, thereby rendering you at once free of the notion of enlightenment and simultaneously enlightened. And that paradoxical state of enlightenment as freedom from enlightenment was my condition at birth, a birth that never was, and I will do my best to get to that birth and the beginning of the book, but now that I have started, it may take me quite a while to get there. The many psychiatrists I have encountered in my life have suggested that I have major issues with beginnings (as well as middles and ends). I think that beginnings suggest to me that there was nothing before what has begun because if there was something before then the beginning would not be a beginning, it would be a continuation. For example, my consciousness is continuous, just like yours, no beginning and no end, and yet people keep insisting that I was born, and I have a great deal of trouble with that, which psychiatrists have called a variety of things from depersonalization to attachment disorder, diagnoses with which I couldn't agree more, but the issue is that they seem to see these as problems, where I see them as solutions.

Have we confused the appearance of a body and the sense that we occupy it with our essential identity? What, then, is it that is cognizant of the apparent body? Does this cognizance disappear when the body does or is it just a change of scene?

Let me put it to you this way: if you are humming along on the road of life and the desert turns to mountains, you could say the scenery has changed but why would you think the driver has changed? It is certainly the beginning of the mountains, but it is not the beginning of the trip. It certainly does not mean that the mountains are driving. It doesn't mean that the mountains were born when I come zooming along or that I should become unhappy when the mountains can no longer be seen, unless of course I cannot see the mountains because it is night and my headlights are not turned on and I crash into a bridge abutment, which would really hurt. And this is why I don't like beginnings, because they turn life inside out and chop it up into pieces that we then become attached to and mourn their end and if we don't get attached to the pieces, but just stay with the continuum, then we have an attachment disorder. In Nosirrah's School of Psychiatry, we have disorders too. We have personality disorder, where a person thinks he exists. We have attachment disorder, where a person becomes attached to a subset of the whole and forgets about the whole itself. In Nosirrah's School of Psychiatry we give drugs to help people hallucinate rather than to help them stop. We give shock treatments to anyone who uses smiley face emoticons in their emails or who talks about integral spirituality. The ground of reality is not the goal of Nosirrah's School of Psychiatry; old psychiatry accomplished that and look where it has gotten us. Our goal is the imagination of what is next. That creative movement is sanity; it has no beginning because it is not in time. Absolute continuity of consciousness is the ending of time and it means that Nosirrah was never born, rather we could say continuous consciousness became extruded into a new form, a form emerging from nothing at all. Nosirrah was born but at the same time I knew that I was not and never had been.

I lived my life backwards, having died just after birth. For one such as me, who lived a lifetime in just days, there was no time to waste because there was no time left. This was not a Merlin life, moving ever younger with a vision of what the future held, but a life so compressed, so dense, that time stopped, breath stopped and all of reality was experienced and then collapsed into itself. The doctors couldn't help, because they ceased to be, the mother's tears didn't fall, there was nothing at all. It was so beautiful, so vast, so undifferentiated that nothing could describe it. Yet it did. Life moved without time or space, and created as that description. Breath moved. Time began. I am, yet I am not. I am, only as a description by the absolute beauty of nothing, the description by the undifferentiated everything.

Mine was a struggle not to transcend life, but to descend into it, a journey not to enlightenment but to the darkest regions of embodiment, the ecstatic tortures of the flesh. For those spiritual acolytes who are struggling to improve yourselves, you can stop now, for when you have finished your perfecting and affecting, your meditating and flagellating, your yoga stretches and your genuflections, your careful diet, careful breathing and, God help you, your careful breeding, and you are the best you that you can be, it won't be enough and it will be too much, it will be sublime but won't be worth a dime, because the best that you will realize now that you are sensitive, quiet, clear and vegan-clean is that, unfortunately for you who have now missed out on years of hedonism and debauchery, what you will realize is that you are still you, and this, my friend, will send you crashing and crawling, collapsing and bawling, down, down, descending down the chakra stairs you so agilely stair-step-machined up, down to the depths of what you transcended, the gunk, the muck, the Maya that is the spiritual DNA of what you are, and you will be so disappointed and depressed that you will give up all spirituality and become cynical, angry and hurt, but nobody in your life will even notice, no one will see you anymore as you now are, in your nasty form, because all they will see is your still lithe, Pilates-stretched body and Rolfed-to-clear eyes, so you will have to start eating meat and stop all bodywork and stop all exercise, drink lots of coffee and watch endless hours of television and obsessively sit in front of the computer and have no more hot-stone massages with salt rub, no manicures, pedicures, in fact, stop even bathing, until you are a bloated, dulled, bloodshot-eyed mess and finally your form will reflect the energy state and those who know you will tsk-tsk and avoid conversation that might lead to the question of what the hell is going on with you, but really what they are avoiding is that energetic state in themselves, and what you might tell them if they did ever ask, which is unlikely, is that their skinny, spiritual bodies and their narrowly spacious, spiritual minds and their ethereal, spiritual spirits can't handle the energy that they are running from, which is why they are running so hard for perfection, and that it is going to be a rough time when the spiritual meets the actual in any life, but of course that is exactly what happens when you are running the spiritual sprint, you run into yourself, the self you left behind when you started, the self you didn't want to be, and like an elevator where the cable has snapped and everyone is screaming, the descent is quick and the result is the destruction of everything and in that destruction lies the freedom from everything and wasn't that what you were looking for when you had the first neurotic thought that you could improve yourself? No, probably not, but there you will be, like Nosirrah, unkempt and smelly, bloodshot eyes, rotting teeth, nails long and cracked, feet so far gone that we cannot begin to describe their condition without causing permanent damage to the reader's peace of mind. No one will give you the time of day, you walk the streets without notice, perhaps drawing a little pity or a bit of disdain. You are no longer a spiritual seeker, nor are you an ordinary person, you have mutated. Here is the thing about rotting teeth, and by metaphoric extension, all putrid and disgusting aspects of the body that result from the destruction of the spiritual self: the rotting teeth spread infection through the bloodstream to the heart, the heart becomes hardened and begins to fail, it is not just the appearance of decrepitude that we begin to manifest when our spiritual quest is destroyed, but we literally experience a broken heart. There is no further down than a heart that has given out, and as the heart falls to pieces we can definitively say that we have hit bottom.

Watching endless hours of television

I will save you the journey, including the falling elevator metaphor and the broken heart metaphor, even though it is a medical reality that rotting teeth can cause congestive heart failure, because what you find out is there is no escape from metaphors and when you try to get rid of that messy, awful self and create the spiritual self, only to collide with the doppelganger of the awful self in a huge, high-speed, head-on, end-over-end collision and ball of fire, splattering ectoplasm everywhere, what you find out is good self, bad self, there isn't any self, just collision, just explosion, just energy. You don't live just to die, or in my case, die just to live, you just aren't and never were. Your broken heart is not yours, it is ours, and this is the great healing and the opening of the way, the discovery that your flailing attempt to escape from yourself and your abject failure at doing so, with its attendant crash and burn collapse, is not your personal heroic journey but the journey of all of humanity through all of history and it is the arising of this very moment, of the creation and destruction of the illusion of reality. There is no escape from Maya, there is no escape from yourself, you don't need to run from the chimera, you don't need to struggle with the myth that is your personal story, you don't need to do anything at all. Your heart is broken, your heart is full, your heart is a metaphor, you are a metaphor, and the metaphor points you to the greatest of compassion for all sentient metaphors. May all metaphors be happy (metaphorically). That is your metaphoric meditation handed down by the great Eddie Buddha some thousand years ago. Eddie was the foremost proponent of Meta-Euphoric Medication, which likely had something to do with eating lotus leaves or possibly smoking them, but nonetheless his teachings became known in Buddhist circles as Meta-phoric Meditation, later shortened when the Americans, one of the Lost Tribes, went to India, Thailand and Burma in the sixties and took over Buddhist marketing, changing the name to the shorter, punchier Meta Meditation, often spelled Metta Meditation. The Americans shortened the meditation itself to "May all beings be happy" and their many students were glad to forget that they were talking metaphorically and began the very serious meditation practice of visualizing each being in the world sitting at their neighborhood Starbucks, gazing into the magic screen of their laptop, accessing their Facebook page and checking "Happy" for current state of mind, while all other beings in the universe Friend them and hit "Like."

Eddie Buddha, rolling over in his grave – well, actually, they burn and scatter the ashes in that part of the world, so he would be rolling in his scattered ashes or something like that, use your imagination and don't make me do all the work here – EB is wondering how the simple contemplation of "the concept is not the actual" that he taught became in modern times the "concept is the actual." Here is what we could explain to him: In modern times Meta has capitulated to Metaphor. In the age of hyper-capitalism we build our lives around Brand.

Now we are at the beginning of the book that thankfully will be published, due to the tireless dedication of Lydia Smythe. She has made it the beginning of the book by excising several hundred pages of pornographic confession because Nosirrah, like St. Augustine, lived a life of carnal degradation, only to realize that this was not the path to follow in a truly spiritual life and the search for God, it wasn't the path to follow, rather it was the path to blaze. I have taken these field notes of the erotic and the profane, chopped from my autobiography, even though these events were the essential expression of my vision, and I have woven them together in a book entitled *Chronic Eros,* which shall be published despite the objections of those who try to control my image while they praise my name and my mystic insight. Lydia, it is not humiliation to appear in the stories of Nosirrah's sexual exploits, it is an honor, and while I know you would rather not see yourself in print, especially the leopard print, the one you so love to wear with your leather, you would rather stay behind the scenes, editing, watching, safe, at least I am not circulating the video of that thing we used to do with the trampoline, the bungee cords and that randy accountant you used to "do your books." *Chronic Eros* is not about you, Lydia, it is about the energy that creates and destroys, the erotic, the uncontrollable in all of us that animates the universe.

Dear Reader, as you peruse these pages and are surprised to find an absence of the quality and quantity of deviant sex that you would normally associate with a spiritual master, please rest assured that the rest of the story can be found in my lurid pornographic masterpiece, *Chronic Eros.* And yes, spiritual masters have far better sex lives than spiritual seekers. The number one rule is that the master can do whatever he wants while the seeker has to follow the rules. The number two rule is that the master makes up the rules. The number three rule is, see the number one rule. That should keep you busy until you are enlightened.

I had to be enlightened early because I had a hard time following normal procedures, not because I was rebellious, but because I was often confused by the instructions that seem to keep coming at me. Like when I try to call into one of those big companies and the computer answering system says, "Do you want to talk to the billing department, say Yes or No" and I say "Yes or No" and the computer person says, "I didn't understand, please say Yes or No" and so I say "Yes or No" and this goes on for hours without much progress. I learned after some experience to start out hitting 2 and then at least I could practice my Spanish. After a while I went for the hearing impaired option, but while I tried to be sensitive to the operator's impairment, she kept saying, "Stop shouting!" I said to her, "Lady, you don't have to shout at me, I'm not the one hard of hearing." It turns out that hearing impaired number is for *customers* who are hard of hearing. I was just trying to be helpful and really this is the crux of the issue in my life. I am so convinced that I am not, that all that there is left to do is to help those who have the horrible fate of thinking that they exist. You could say I was born with this purpose, except what is not is not born, and come to think of it, purpose would be a gross exaggeration of Nosirrah's non-existence.

You may wonder what I mean by non-existence, so let me explain. We exist only in our concept of our self; that concept is itself just a form of resistance to the vast nothingness that awaits the silence of the mind. We maintain our busy life of the mind as a kind of anxiety about our emptiness, and that anxiety is what we think of as our self. We say we want peace, but peace is the end of anxiety, and therefore the end of the self. So what we really want is to want peace, not to have it, because wanting peace is more anxiety and therefore more self. To end wanting peace and to simply be peace is to be nothing and that is a fearless state, or rather, a fearless non-state. Nosirrah has known this fearless state since birth. I was without fear and this seemed to make those around me quite fearful. I was taken to priests and rabbis, healers and psychics, psychiatrists and podiatrists, and all other forms of doctors. After much consultation and collaboration, I was not declared enlightened, rather I was declared to have a rare genetic disorder, Urbach-Wiethe disease. I had lesions on my amygdala, preventing me from experiencing any normal fear of terror-inducing hauntings and demons, ghosts and monsters, death threats, being attacked, snakes, spiders, none of these had any effect on me at all and since my childhood was full of all of these things, I had a pretty normal childhood.

But one thing in my childhood concerned me: if I had no fear, then how could I transcend fear and become enlightened? As a spiritual prodigy, at an early age I had read all the religious texts, *The Bible*, *The Koran*, *The Bhaga-vad-Gita*, *Tao de Ching*, and all the spiritual classics, over and over. I read in the original Latin and contemplated A.E. Walinbrucke's *Verum Nihilim*, which makes all other books on human consciousness look like marginal postscripts, but I read on nonetheless, *The Necronomicon*, *The Book of the Damned*, *Being One*, *Tales from the Crypt* comics, and more. Later in life, I came upon the spawn of the New Age, books that told me to be in the now, then to be love, to be peaceful, to be mindful. But these books just brought one question to me over and over again: if I was supposed to be something other than what I was, what was I? I realized that this was a question that was neither present nor loving, peaceful nor mindful, in short, I realized that I was alive and was surrounded by the spiritual undead, zombies, spiritual zombies practicing zombie spirituality. You may ask how you can tell if you are alive or a zombie, let me explain.

Is there an emptiness in you that cannot be filled without endless, mindless feasting on the living? Do you have no purpose other than consumption, and yet there is no fulfilling the hunger? Do you stagger, grasping, clawing, irrespective of the damage it does to your own ravaged being, driven to feed, without knowing why, without even the question of why as a possibility? Is the drive to possess, to fill yourself all that you know? Are you a spiritual zombie?

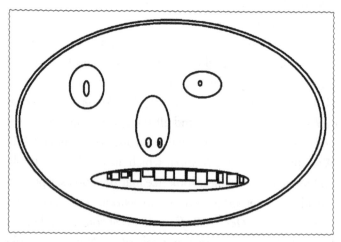

Spiritual zombie

Look around you. Do you see a shelf of books on spirituality and self-improvement? Does your credit card bill reflect
enrollment in seminars, workshops, retreats or even on-line
meditation groups? Do you feel that your understanding is
not enough, that your stress level is too high, that there is
something missing in your life, that happiness is available
to everyone but you? Are you going to classes where you
stretch your ligaments, work on your core strength or pretend to be boxing while jumping up and down? Do you use
words from ancient languages, gestures from cultures and
religions alien to your own, and read translations of ancient
texts as if these are instructions directed towards you?

These are just some of the beginning signs of spiritual
zombification, a kind of viral infection that is passed easily
from the lurching zombie to you. At first you didn't notice,
a friend gave you an amazing book to read, or took you
to see an insightful teacher, or convinced you to do a yoga
weekend. This seemed innocent enough. But, soon the virus
began to spread to your central nervous system, and the first
symptoms began to appear almost unnoticed (one of which
was that you began to refer to your central nervous system
as your chakras). You began to believe that there was the
possibility of enlightenment now, or enlightenment next,
or enlightenment in a previous incarnation, but whatever
that enlightenment thing was, you wanted it, you deserved
it and you were going to get it. The zombie begins to have
strange appetites. Sprout salad with a side of tofu begins
to look like a tasty meal despite the intensive gas buildup
in your third chakra (which is probably just a little energy
movement). Books that were written for total morons begin

to look profound. Even this book, which was written by a total madman, may seem weighty.

And speaking of weighty, the zombie not only reads spiritual books but also "understands," although the zombie's not always holding the books right side up, but for zombies these books make sense. They consist of an amalgam of all philosophies randomly cut and pasted into a chart of quadrants, levels, and fields, although all the fields are left fields (way out in left field) and published in immense volumes (see weighty) with the conclusionary tautology that if you understand and agree with the conclusion then you are at the highest state of consciousness and if you find the writings to be derivative ramblings that are unreadable, unintelligible and jargoned, then you are at a lower state of consciousness and cannot understand the conclusion anyway.

Think of it as astrology for the thinking zombie, or as a kind of technical stock trading system using charts and graphs – both result in a random success rate, but what we like to remember is the successes and what we like to forget are the failures. If you throw enough material in a book, even zombies will recognize something in that mass of information that resonates with their experience and the rest of the material just fades into the background. The trick is to make those books big, and then the zombie master has a career explaining it to his fellow automatons. Those who don't get the teaching get eaten. Wait, don't eat me, and then spit me out into the mouths of your followers like a mother robin feeding her young! Yuck.

One of these teachers can produce No Brain Activity at will and has a YouTube clip to show it. He does this while awake! No brain activity while awake – isn't that great! And he did this with a special and rare form of meditation. It is everlasting awareness. Now that is marketing!

But, let us for just one minute engage our minds and remain awake, and I know this may be difficult for many of you (and no, you cannot turn on the television to keep your mind engaged). This will only take a minute. Engage your mind and follow this deductive reasoning:

All zombies have no brain activity and appear to be awake.

Human beings who are awake have brain activity and consider that quite acceptable, usually even desirable.

Human beings without brain activity are considered clinically dead.

A spiritual teacher has no brain activity when he is awake and has proudly placed video evidence of this on YouTube.

Therefore, the spiritual teacher is a zombie.

Quod Erat Demonstrandum.

For those of you who are not used to dealing with the kind of high level mathematical logic that I have just utilized to prove my point, let me say it in plain language: the teacher is awake but dead and he wants you to join his group of undead.

Inspired by this awesome demonstration of Sahaja Nir-vikalpa Samadhi, I realized I have something to offer the world similar to this mind that doesn't think. I have a flaccid body with virtually no muscle tone and barely the capacity to walk around the block. I did this by sitting around doing nothing. I would like to produce a YouTube video on this but have found a great deal of resistance to filming me with my shirt off, something to do with obscenity laws and local standards. My promise is that you, too, can have everlasting lack of muscle tone with my special meditation, found in my forthcoming book tentatively titled *Sex, Ecology and More Sex: A Brief History of Everything Else Except That Too Complicated Integral Stuff*. I put the word *ecology* in there because it is good to be green, although I am not really too eco-logically aware myself, except I do collect aluminum cans when I am short on cash, which is pretty frequently, but if you aren't really green then it is really good to pretend you are. It sells things to other people who are pretending that they are green. Real green people don't buy things and that makes for lousy book sales.

I put the word *sex* in there twice because it is twice as important as any other word, even green people will buy something with sex attached to it and I am hoping some really stunning integral lady gets the hint that the word *sex* and everything it represents on all levels, all quadrants and all positions is important to me (except the position where I am bending over backwards touching my heels, that is a little hard on my back with Ms. Integral bouncing around) and even though I don't have a cool loft apartment like the hip integralists, I would be OK in the back seat of my car, which is kind of like a loft, lots of glass and steel, good urban street view. I will have to move all my clothes and canned dog food out of the way (no, I don't have a dog), but it is already set up with a sleeping bag.

But Nosirrah has one teensy, weensy insight, an insight that exists just at the outer edge of Everything, it is a known, so it is part of the Everything, but is paradoxically an unknown and so it is not part of anything. Here it is in summary: what is not known is infinitely more than what is known, and while it is impressive to endlessly rehash what is known, the true explorer heads for the unknown, where few go and the pay is not very good.

My book will be about the things I would like to know a lot more about, in other words mostly Sex, but I will reserve a certain amount of my eloquent prose for what is beyond the edge of Everything, the vast and untrod regions of Everything Else. And I will do it in under 100 pages, perhaps even in a pamphlet. Eventually I hope to have my own *Pocket N. Nosirrah,* a compilation of all the profound wisdom I have acquired over the many years of spiritual inquiry, the totality of which will not fit on thousands of pages or in dozens of books, but will encompass the infinite, ineffable whole and as such it will fit easily in the pocket because the knowing of the whole leaves no knower behind to write a single word. Is there anything that fits more easily in the pocket than nothing at all?

If you are a spiritual zombie there is no point in trying to understand or to change. The spiritual zombie has no capacity for such things, because the spiritual zombie is not alive, it is simply spiritual. Spiritual is hunger, hunger looks for truth, which is a kind of food; truth is what is alive, but which is made dead in the feeding. The spiritual zombie must kill what is alive to feed its spirituality. In turn, what is alive must kill the spiritual, and with it, the zombie.

Consider this book as advice to you if you are a spiritual zombie, so that you may survive the onslaught of the few who are still alive. You are many, and while you are blinded by your hunger, perhaps you will come upon this book, not that it will awaken you from your spirituality, but perhaps it will be of use to you in understanding why what is alive must destroy you, despite your spirituality, your meditation, your incense and yoga mat.

But *Sex, Ecology and More Sex: A Brief History of Everything Else Except That Too Complicated Integral Stuff* is primarily for those few who are alive and who must survive the spiritual zombies. For you there is the possibility of escaping the infection, and while your aliveness will destroy the spiritual zombies as you make contact, it is not hatred or fear that does the destruction, but the vitality and creativity of the life force.

Those readers who are familiar with my end-of-the-world self-help book, *2013: How to Profit from the Prophets in the Coming End of the World,* will recall that I turned down the title *The Secret Power of Love, Sex, Money and Weight Loss Guaranteed with the Ancient Tibetan Yoga Zen Way of Crystals* despite my expertise in the areas of Love and Sex and my transcendence of the area of Money, for the singular reason that I knew nothing about Weight Loss and had, as a result, become quite plump. While the title would sell the book, the book would not transform the reader, and I refused to use it. I also briefly considered calling it *You Are Greedy and Narcissistic, but Don't Worry About It Because It Is All Illusion Anyway,* which is pretty great, you have to admit.

While the title *Sex, Ecology and More Sex* IS brilliant, I realized that *The Secret Power of Love, Sex, Money and Weight Loss* is stronger because Ecology makes people think about recycling and compact fluorescent bulbs, and let's face it, even if we print it on recycled paper with soy ink, it isn't going to sell.

You may wonder why the title I refused for the last book is now being discussed at all. I will tell you, but first, I would like to address those who have not read my prior books. To you first-time readers, if I were a man of gentle nature and good manners, I would say welcome to our small community of inquirers, a kind of club for those who have discovered enough to know that they will never discover enough. I would, if I were a man of social graces, say to those who have never picked up a book of mine before, please come in, sit and rest, have a warm cup of chamomile tea while we discuss the mysterious nature of life and the truth found dead center in the human heart. And since you are a reader who has never chanced upon my obscure but perhaps unparalleled writings, you would have no way of knowing that I do not possess a gentle nature, nor manners of any kind, nor would you know that there is no club and no inquiry, therefore nothing to discuss, and most importantly, as to chamomile tea, you would not know anything in particular about chamomile tea since this is the first time it has appeared in any of my works and it does so as a fully conscious act on the part of this writer because what you did not know until this moment is that chamomile tea contains coumarin, which has appetite-suppressing properties, and while that may seem like a fine thing and a key bit of information in a book about weight loss, you might not realize that where there is yin there is yang, and this same delightful herb that can help you to a new, thinner body can, in larger amounts, have a deleterious effect on your liver and kidneys, and in yet larger amounts will kill rats, and eventually you. You will not be having a cup of chamomile tea with me, nor will your rats. And, now that I have cleared up any fantasies that you, as a new reader, may be having about our relationship, I do suggest that you purchase and read all of my prior books as well as my future books, so that I do not have to continue to explain to you what you will and will not be experiencing. If you insist on continuing to read this book without making the investment in these other books, which will pay me a small pittance of royalty, I cannot guarantee that my rent will be paid and therefore I cannot guarantee that this book will be finished, and even if finished, that it will be even remotely comprehensible.

As I was saying to those who have read my prior books, you may be wondering why I have once again mentioned *The Secret Power of Love, Sex, Money and Weight Loss*, a title I had clearly rejected. The title was test marketed by the publisher, who discovered an astounding 93 percent of potential readers would buy it immediately, even if they had to sell themselves on the streets to raise the cover price, and data indicated that there were millions of such potential readers. Unfortunately, what was not understood at the time was that those millions were in such poor mental and physical condition that nobody would want to buy them on the street or anywhere else for that matter. Otherwise, my readers were largely broke and therefore could not afford to buy books of any sort. This showed me that, more than ever, this title was needed by my readers, albeit at a much reduced price. Also, I decided to join a fitness club to get in shape, and found my way to 25 Hour Fitness, whose motto is "Fitness for those who don't have enough time in their day," a business that seemed to be generating large profits, and I use the word *generating* intentionally, since 25 Hour Fitness doesn't make money on its membership fees, but rather on connecting all the treadmills to generators and selling the electricity back to the community. Before they hit on the electrical generating scheme, they sold memberships at a slight loss and presumed they would make it up on volume; after all, it is a fitness club, not a genius club.

People at these workout places exercise like it was a funeral. The workout places are very serious, very focused, slightly funky odor like your Aunt Agatha when she pats you on the head and says she is very sorry about your loss, very much like a funeral, except everyone is wearing shorts or spandex. I am not that serious, I am rarely focused, but I do have the funky odor part down, I guess I am just a natural.

There are treadmills where you run and pretend that you are getting somewhere, dripping sweat the whole time. Weight machines that are essentially medieval torture devices. Free weights are available so that you can snap numerous ligaments and tendons. And when you are dripping with sweat, bleeding from the cuts, and various pusses and lymphatic drainages are oozing out, then just jump in the pool for a quick rinse off.

After a visit to 25 Hour Fitness

OK, I will admit that I am making this all up. It is not that I couldn't imagine a club that would have me as a member, I just can't imagine joining a club that would expect their members to exercise, although truthfully I do like to exercise my member and that is quite enough exercise for me.

I will also admit that this is not a book about losing weight, although if you do want to lose weight here is the secret: exercise more, eat less, get rid of all mirrors and stop thinking you exist. This is the essence of the Nosirrah Low Fat, Low Protein, Low Sugar, Low Carb, but Eat Anything You Want When Nobody Is Looking Because If You Stop Thinking About It You Don't Exist Anyway Diet. In short, non-existence doesn't weigh anything at all and can eat whenever and whatever it wants. You think you are, then you think you shouldn't, but then you think you have just polished off a quart of Chunky Monkey and then you think you are fat. This is a narrative, a story of mind, the invisible string of the pearls of thoughts made into a fine and shiny necklace so enthralling that you forget that it is made up of imaginary pearls, strung with imaginary string into an imaginary necklace. You are a very plump, full-of-ice-cream necklace that doesn't look at all like the pictures in the fashion magazines. But, here is where it gets really sweet (and yes, that word is intended to trigger a desire to go for another round of Chunky Monkey). It is sweet because those ultrathin, grim looking models in the fashion magazines do not exist either. Of course, they think they do exist, and they think they are fat.

Nevertheless, I was going to get healthy, even if it killed me. And death, after all, is the real topic of all books, all spirituality, all religion. It is simply that we avoid facing this topic, using love, sex, money and weight loss as attempts to avoid what we will inevitably face. I can tell you how you can be rid of your addiction to love, sex, money and weight loss all at once, in just a moment, without spiritual practices, without psychological counseling, in fact without any effort at all. In my forthcoming book, which will now be entitled *The Secret Power of Love, Sex, Money and Weight Loss,* I will tell you how to do this at the end of the book and you should not under any circumstances go to the end of the book to read the secret, thereby saving yourself the economic sacrifice of buying the book and the arduous task of reading the book. Look for it soon, and until then, you will need to complete the book you have in your hand, which will no doubt leave you clamoring for more.

Editor's Note:

Nosirrah's book entitled *Sex, Ecology and More Sex: A Brief History of Everything Else Except That Too Complicated Integral Stuff* and retitled *The Secret Power of Love, Sex, Money and Weight Loss Guaranteed with the Ancient Tibetan Yoga Zen Way of Crystals* is unlikely to ever be published, primarily due to the lack of a finished manuscript or really a manuscript of any kind, unless you consider stacks of scribblings on paper napkins a manuscript, and the fact that we cannot currently locate the author, however, I have published here the end of this book referred to in the above paragraph in the hopes of bringing some continuity to the current book. My hope is that the reader will forgive the apparently disjointed flow of the prose of this book and focus instead on the kernels of profound insight hidden away in the jumble of non-sequiturs. I can assure you that I share your frustration. If any reader does locate Nosirrah, please contact me immediately, and most importantly, understand that the glazed eyes and rigid body does NOT mean he is dead, this is the deep meditation of Samadhi, where all senses are withdrawn from the outer world, so do not cremate without contacting me and, no, that smell is not the overpowering stench of a corpse left too long in the sun, that is his normal fragrance. I often compare Nosirrah's odor to a billy goat, and I would do so here except for a strongly worded cease-and-desist letter from the American Goat Society claiming defamation. You may recall that billy goats urinate on their front legs and beards during rutting season to attract the females, sometimes adding farts to the mix for that added malodorous edge, and in general billy goats are known for their unbearable odor and their unrelenting libido. I can well understand how comparing Nosirrah's aroma and randiness to that of these remarkable beasts would be defaming to the noble goats and I will certainly refrain from such comparisons. The part about the front legs and beards was remarkably similar though, one must admit. Thank you.

—*Lydia Smyth*

Here are the final paragraphs of the forthcoming work referenced above:

In the introduction to this book I promised that at the end I would reveal how you will free yourself of your attachment, your obsessions with love, sex, money and weight loss. Did I mention that these are all an avoidance of the direct look at death?

You will be free when you look death directly in the eye and embrace that finality, a finality that is not in some future, and is not now, but a death that has already happened. You will be free when you are not. You will be free in a moment, and that moment will be celebrated at your funeral because most will not recognize it until then. Your liberation is the strange gift of death – great intensification, total mystery, raw emotion without any resolution and the relentless ongoingness of everything else as if nothing has happened at all, which is the paradoxical aspect, that, in fact, nothing at all has happened.

Author's Note:

Lydia Smythe has asked me to refocus as she feels that this book is meandering and is without any central theme. She does not appear to understand the literary symbolism of this lack of apparent direction.

Remember, this is an autobiography of the life of a
mystic. This mystic's realization, his teaching, the
expression of the very fabric of his being is that Life
is meandering and has no central theme. This is bril-
liantly represented in the structure of this book, which
is itself a metaphor of the enlightened state. In addi-
tion, I do enjoy what the psychiatrists term "thought
disorder," which can mean derailment of thoughts,
tangentiality, incoherence, illogicality, neologisms,
perseveration, stilted speech, echolalia, and I believe
that all of these are well represented in my writing, in
my writing, writing, lighting, biting writing. But, my
friends, if you look very closely at your own thoughts,
speech and writing, you will find that you, too, suffer
from the association of thought to thought and that
the sum of all your loosely associated thinking is not
only tangential but also entirely incoherent except to
itself and represents the worst possible case of echolalia, where you don't just simply echo your thoughts,
but that these thoughts are themselves only echoes of
what you have heard, been taught or been told by the
social structures of your life, those social structures,
of course, being made of the same echoes. As I said, I
enjoy this thought disorder as it gives me the sense of
a noisy jungle with all the sounds of a thousand beasts,
without apparent purpose other than the vocalization.
It is a symphony of meaninglessness and in that there
is beauty. But you, poor reader, you struggle with

your thought disorder, you try to carve out purpose and meaning from acausality, a struggle for a central theme in your life that will occupy your waking life and your dream world, with the brief moments of pure consciousness in deep sleep as your only respite, a break in your thought disorder, which you do not remember and so for you it does not exist. Stop looking for meaning and learn to enjoy the ennui, appreciate your thoughts as they derail and then begin to perseverate again; thoughts are noise, thoughts are music, thoughts are not what you are, or where you are going, or the why or how of the universe, no matter how perverse or how beautiful they appear to be.

Thoughts are empty, just as you are, and you can relax now, even though your thoughts cannot. Your thoughts have a thought disorder, you are fine. This, too, my friend, is the encoded message in the very structure of the literary work you hold in your hands. Now it is decoded, enjoy the rest of the pages.

But I have digressed from the very purpose of this book, which is to tell the story of my life. In my chef d'oeuvre, *God Is An Atheist*, I revealed that I was the bastard son of Franz Kafka and Alice B. Toklas and was raised in the salon apartment in Paris of Gertrude Stein, ignored by Stein and Toklas as they tried to ignore the fling that Alice had had with Kafka, despite her arrangement with Stein. Kafka was never much of a father for that matter, mainly because he died before I was born. I grew up in denial, the denial that I was at all. This was Gertrude's greatest gift to me, as I came to see that she was right, I was not Alice's child, nor did I live in Gertrude's apartment.

This is the difficult aspect of autobiography, which is that I don't remember my childhood and I am not sure that it happened. Did I grow up in Gertrude Stein's apartment, I don't speak French for example, comment pourrait j'avoir grandi à Paris? My first psychiatrist insisted that I was the son of the long established Nosirrah family of Albrightsville, PA, but I can't remember exactly his rationale for that assertion, nor can I remember him, although I do recall that he did like to do those shock treatments and his name was Dr. French, je suis confus, is this memory or construction looking for coherence? Perhaps the doctor's name was Felsenfeld, not French, and I was born of common parents, not great literary figures, and simply suffered not of neglect but of affluence, the abuse of too much attention, too many things, and too many expectations. Perhaps my parents were a good and kind couple who cared for me the best they could within the constraints of their own understanding and limitations. Perhaps there was no one to blame, not even Dr. French or Felsenfeld or whatever his name was. The worst of this bland possibility of overwhelming and smothering normalcy is that it would have cursed me with the absence of a childhood plotline to point to, to write about, to rely on for the accreditation of a literary back story.

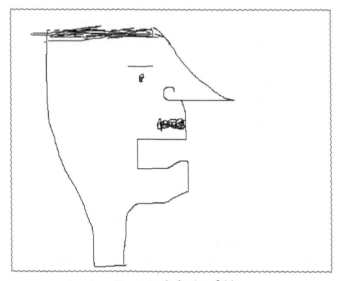

Dr. French/Felsenfeld

The weight of this vanilla childhood must have been too great, the unending expanse of ordinary, where excellent is average even if it isn't very good and trophies are handed out just for showing up and "great job" is the mantra of every enlightened parent. I had to create an alternative world where tension existed, failure was possible, pain was not always relieved. That is why I was taken to the psychiatrist's office, to be adjusted back to the median. They didn't realize that a long gestating disassociation with myself had given birth to a no-mind no-me, they didn't realize that I once was found but now was lost, was mind, but now, not me. I had vanished and no psychiatrist could reconstitute a boy who never was, and that story is the one I can now tell because it is the one I wrote, and having written it, I can certify to you without any doubt that I lived it. I have erased what was written in the book of life and scribbled over it with the stubs of pencils too short to fit into the hand of a schoolboy and the near empty cartridges of pens discarded on the sidewalk, scribbled the mad prose of a life without a center and without any excuse except to risk a total life. This is the fourth book of life, one not commonly acknowledged, for our Western religions teach three books – there is the Book of Life, where God sees your good deeds and gives you life everlasting, there is the Book of Death, in which your evil deeds send you to a Lake of Fire, and if your deeds are not that clear, then there is the Benonim, it is the book of suspended sentences, with a year to work out your errors before the books are read once more. These three books are referenced in the Bible, the Talmud and holy books back to Babylonia. But, there is a fourth book unmentioned in any religious writings, it is the book of the mystic who transcends all form. It cannot be found in the Babylonian scriptures, nor in the Jewish Jubilees, nor in the biblical Chapter of Revelations. This is the book of Nosirrah, the book of the one who leaves no trace, who makes no act, who does no deeds and creates no karma. This is my book, written in a hand unsteady and unsure even of the letters it makes to form the words that make the story, a story with no beginning and no ending and no substance at all but what the reader, not the writer, conjures as its content. Nosirrah is of this fourth book, and you, dear reader, shall make of it only what you have the capacity to see – do look deeply and clearly, for what you see is what you are, not in an afterlife of heaven or hell, not next year when you can try again, but what you are, what you already are, a priori. This is not just the autobiography of Nosirrah, but it is your autobiography, too. You, too, write your story in the infirm hand of memory and projection, looking to establish yourself in the ever shifting sands of reality – reality, it might be added, created entirely by the grains of sand, the moments of thought, all moving, blowing about as if it is the ground of our being, when we know it is not. There is no ground of being, just shift. Shift happens. That is the meaning of life.

You are like a pointillist painter, placing dot after dot on the canvas of your life in the hopes that when you step back you will see a clear and beautiful picture. But what if when you step back you see only dots? Or worse, you see only the space between the dots? The dots are information, the space is exformation, and together they are totality, a unitary whole without form, and hence without any reality. We know the dots, we don't know the space, and in the angst of that unknowing, we create a narrative from what we know, and this suggests to us that the dots are of great value. Crisis tends to jolt this value, or perhaps we could say that when the value in the information is jolted we create the story of a crisis. Crisis is when you look at your life and you just see dots, no connection, no picture, no space, no unity, just dots. Psychology helps you by assisting you in seeing the picture that the dots make up, spirituality helps you by showing you the space between the dots, and, if you are lucky, your psychological and spiritual search will be resolved by seeing the dots and the space and the picture and one big formless mess and then letting out a blood curdling scream which will wake the museum guard from his stupor and he will escort you out of the gallery and onto the street, where you can wander aimlessly for the rest of your days without worrying about dots, space or the pictures they form. That is the freedom from metaphor, which may be the ultimate freedom.

After my childhood, which I have described above, which was rich in experience, idyllic in an abusive sort of way, I was left, as a young adult, entirely enlightened and ready to teach. The problem was I couldn't find a student. I didn't have the most prestigious address, mostly alleys, occasionally a park bench. It is true that my message was somewhat advanced, basically, undo and don't ask questions, there are no answers. The people I met wanted to know what kind of yoga we would be doing, or was this tantric meditation, or would it work to try this for a half an hour in the morning. I drove those spiritual tourists off with a stick. No student came. But I taught anyway, mostly to spiritual tourists before I drove them off. Since I was enlightened, this seemed the best thing to do. Enlightenment is great. It is highly recommend to all spiritual seekers. It is grand to come to the fruition of all the confrontation of conditioning, the exploration of both the sublime states and the attachments to money and sex. It is particularly nice when others see that you have got it, and then whatever you do or say becomes a teaching moment. Nothing really beats the experience of enlightenment, or the non-experience if you want to get technical.

Spiritual tourist

The main problem with enlightenment is post-enlightenment. What was profound becomes trite, what was subtle becomes obvious, what was new becomes old. You realize that whatever the enlightenment was, it isn't. Maybe it never was. You can't really know that, but you can know that now it isn't. Those hanging on your every enlightened word assume that the enlightenment that now isn't, still is. No matter what you say or do, they still organize it as enlightened speech and action. You tell them there is no enlightenment, you mock yourself, you mock them, you fail to say anything wise or even vaguely useful. No one hears. There are no students, just tourists.

This is a hell world. You are respected, maybe even revered. You can't change that. No one hears. So you stop talking.

Silence is the great screen for the projector of the mind. Not speaking excites the mind to run its movies on fast forward. Silence doesn't destroy the notion of enlightenment, it reinforces it. The tourists love silence, they can produce their own movie, but eventually they get bored.

So you stop speaking, stop moving from alley to park bench, stop responding to inquiries. Slowly, the tourists wander off to find a new focus for the enlightenment story. You are left alone at last and you fade into the obscurity that has been the truth all along.

The end of Nosirrah's enlightenment came swiftly and good riddance. Enlightenment is a lot of pressure, with too many people watching for signs of human weakness, and so I developed facial tics, myofascial pain and generalized horniness, and taking care of the latter seemed to cure all the formers. Not that I am obsessed or anything, but sex does seem to solve a lot of problems and in this case not only were my various psychosomatic illnesses gone, but so was any illusion of enlightenment, due to the fact that we video recorded that Inner Circle of Disciples meeting where we worked on trust issues by trusting that removing all clothes and jumping into bed together would be really fun and then got that video mixed up with the video "The Importance of Celibacy for Meditators" we were supposed to be showing to that large group at the intro seminar. People were horrified, not by the randy gymnastics between Nosirrah and his six closest disciples, a Cirque du Soleil level performance sans costumes that belied pretty much all the teachings so far and suggested not just that Nosirrah was a weak human but that he was a pretty kinky weak human, although quite flexible and apparently double jointed in some interesting anatomical areas, but what horrified the audience, well you would have to see that large hairy mole that takes up most of my back to understand just how horrified an audience could be, although it does look something like that burnt toast image of Jesus in a hairy mole sort of way and for a perceptive few there was a strong ecstatic experience on the other side of the horror, something like the feeling of digestive peace one feels after expelling listeria-laced food from one's belly by violently retching, but nevertheless, old devotional video clips of it can still be found on YouTube, I think under "hairy mole" or maybe "hairy mole Jesus cures" or something like that. Speaking of moles that dig in the ground in family groups, it is said that when you have a line of moles digging through the earth, the first one is smelling the food they are searching for but the last one only smells molasses. That, of course, is a different sort of mole, but worthy of mention in case there are any middle schoolers reading through this, unsupervised by their parents. For the parents: mole asses, get it? God, you are thick.

But, I digress from what is an essential topic, which is to say, Nosirrah's hairy mole as a signifier of his mystic nature. I am sure you are well aware that for the early pagan Arabs, a hairy mole on the back was considered an important sign of a prophet, an indicator of a great shaman who could control the forces of nature. There is some debate whether Mohammed himself had a hairy mole on his back, a Seal of the Prophets. I want to make clear that Nosirrah's hairy mole has nothing to do with Arabic culture, pagan or present, or the Islamic faith, and that it does not suggest that Nosirrah is a prophet, nor put him in conflict with those Muslims who believe that Mohammed was the final prophet, or for that matter those Muslims who believe that Mohammed was *not* the final prophet, and further, the form of Jesus is clearly identifiable in the hairy mole mass, so even if Nosirrah is a prophet by accident, he would be more in the Christian department, although this is not to suggest that he is a Christian either because that is going to activate a whole bunch of fundamentalistas who are going to attack him as the Anti-Christ, which he is also not, and just to be clear that just because he is denying he is the Anti-Christ he is most definitely not claiming to be the Second Coming, it is just that his mole looks like Jesus but could be another olive skinned, bearded man in his mid-thirties who happens to be beatific and convey miraculous healings through the mere regarding of the hairy mole even if you just view it on You-Tube, and further, Nosirrah, with regards to his hairy mole, its healing powers and his prophetic credentials, makes no claims, representations or warranties about any religion past or future. I don't mean to be mole-ier than thou, but I predict with certainty, yes, I prophesy that this will be the end of the matter of my being a prophet. If I am wrong, then I am right, and, of course, if I am right, then obviously I am right.

In any event, the video mix-up scandal took care of my enlightenment. I was free, not enlightened, but free. But, what do you do with freedom when you are not enlightened? I knew that what was next had to be practical and use the skill set that had gotten me this far – obsession. Practical obsession, the guiding principal of my new life.

Obsessive thought is fascinating at every level and functionally debilitating, but I could see clearly that functioning is a criterion that is socially constructed. The desire to understand or change this obsessive behavior creates a potent relationship to those with insight. When you go to another for that insight do you want the phenomenon to change or do you want understanding of the phenomenon? Transformation of consciousness and transmutation of fear are possible outcomes of the most challenging of conditions, but for most the desire is to find security and safety in functionality regardless of what is left hidden. When we are the helper, are we helping the other to understand or to adjust so they can function? Each of us has to understand what perspective we are looking from when we reach out to help to see if we are helping at all. Many tried to help me, but few knew where they were helping from. Mine was the search for understanding and transformation; functioning was never my strong suit.

It is a funny thing that we think about thinking so much, even though thought is insubstantial, even this sentence, which reflects a thought about thought. Phenomenology is endless, the expansive, the micro, the sublime, the crude. While we may try to categorize it, control it, find our place in it, the form through which we try to understand the universe is not the universe as it is. So the task that your mind has set for itself will never end, whether you struggle with it or not, but neither will it have actuality in its struggle. That we live in inner or outer drama suggests that we have an aversion for the emptiness that awaits us when we no longer struggle; the practicality of obsession is that it takes us to the end of itself.

Draw the distinction between the phenomenon and the description of the phenomenon, and notice that the description can become a social construction within which the phenomenon is assigned a good or bad quality. Speaking from the most basic perspective, the phenomenological, there is no distinction between socially acceptable and socially deviant occurrences, and this is the deep perspective I have found myself exploring, a kind of Tantric OCD world that has no restraints but also no motivations, like finding yourself at an all-you-can-eat buffet with no appetite, everything is possible but there is no impulse to create anything. Those who walked by me on the streets were not experiencing their life fundamentally but rather as it is socially constructed, where certain behaviors are clearly better than others. They are lost in the fallacy of occupying only the social construct rather than the whole perspective from phenomenological to social. If I was occupying the whole, was it possible to convey to those I met the chance for the expansion of perspective, was it possible to be a modern day Bodhisattva, a contemporary avatar, a bright-born whose unflagging compassion transforms all whom he meets?

Maybe it was possible, but I didn't find out, because I was distracted by a rather attractive woman whose come hither look made me come hither and, boy, did I end up in the hither. She was, as Frank Sinatra warned me when I first glanced at her, a witch. I was hanging with my buddy Frank, who knew this look and this woman all too well, he had seen it a million times at a million stage doors, and he warned me, in a rather harsh voice I might add, screaming at me to resist the witch, but it was too late, sorry Frank, I was already under her spell. Frank capitulated and just started singing.

Frank Sinatra

Imagine, if you can, Frank Sinatra mockingly singing his song "Witchcraft" in the background as I was drawn deep into the web of this she-demon:

> Those fingers in my hair,
> that sly come hither stare,
> that strips my conscience bare,
> it's witchcraft.

You see, my dear readers, in those young days I did actually have hair, and Beloved had gazed at me from across the room and held my eyes in hers. The come hither stare works on a deep biological level, suggesting to us that the other is ready, willing and able to mate. We call that love, because "rutting ritual" has too many letters for one of those heart pendants. I was magnetized by the held gaze, but the coup de grâce was the contraction of her facial muscles, resulting in the slight upturning of the corners of her mouth, something we refer to as a smile, which I am told suggests that a person is happy. There is ample research that suggests that this smile amplifies the power of the come hither stare, sealing the deal; the combination is nearly overwhelming in the suggestion of genetic combining and so it worked well, forcing me to cross the room, hypnotized by the notion that I was loved, and then in an instant I placed my hair upon her fingers, just the way Frank instructed me from among the various voices within my head. No, Frank Sinatra was not with me in that bar, it was his spirit in my head, along with all the other spirit people that yell at me there, telling me to do things I don't really want to do.

It was only later that I found out that Beloved was looking at someone behind me, but by that time I had entangled her hand so thoroughly in my dreads that she was completely distracted from the man she had actually been attracted to, and was entirely focused on getting her rings, bracelet and three fingers and a thumb extracted from my matted locks (there apparently had been an industrial accident, resulting in the short count on the fingers).

Since I had always had difficulty with social perceptions and interpersonal relationships due to the fact that I had deconstructed the social mores I was conditioned with, and then lost most of the pieces, I have never been too sure how to relate to a woman. I knew that I had to relate in order to have sex, so I knew relating was important, and I had studied a guide to dating published in the peer reviewed scientific journal *Psychological Science* entitled "Integrating gaze direction and expression in preferences for attractive faces" and so I knew very well that dilated pupils, fixed gaze held for more than a few seconds, and upturned corners of mouth meant rutting ritual, so it must be love.

By the time we got the hand untangled, using sheep shears that she happened to have at her apartment to cut through the matted hair, we were re-entangled in a Heisenberg principal sort of way. She had me in her spell and soon I found that I was to be a father and to live a normal life in suburbia and occupy myself with gainful employment, that my eyes were only for her, and the shears would be kept at close hand in case my eyes wandered. It turned out that they were not wool shears but gelding shears.

The days of rutting ritual were over, and the rutting began, ruthless, relentless rutting. The result was A. Nosirrah and B. Nosirrah. This is not a *Cat in the Hat* allusion, these are the offspring of Nosirrah, carrying the mystic bloodline and therefore born tulkus. They were teachers come to this plane to kick ass, and I was their only student. Because the rutting had ended once A and B were popped out of the oven, I had plenty of time on my hand, no pun intended.

I will recount in greater detail the raising of these two twice born in my parenting guide, *Nosirrah's Guide to Raising Children: If You Can't Join Them, Beat Them.*

Here is the thing about children, unless you actively attempt to destroy them they seem to do all right on their own. That is because they are not children, they are life, just as you are life. You are not raising a child, you are a field of consciousness in which your form and the child's protrudes.

Have you given birth? If not, perhaps you have been born? In either case, you have experienced the field of consciousness extruding form, field and form are not two but one, mother and child are not two but one. Mother, father, children, dog, hamster, minivan, all One. Unpaid mortgage, girlfriend, wife's hyper-aggressive divorce attorney, girlfriend's irate husband and his Glock 9mm with 17 rounds are all One, just field pushing out form. How does field raise field, how does parent raise child? There is nothing to do because there is everything to do and if you relate to everything, nothing will get done, and anyway it is all getting done by field, so you can relax.

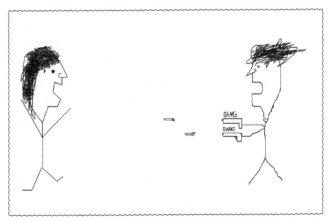

Girlfriend's irate husband with his Glock 9mm

Parenting is where we get to exhibit the best of ourselves and the rest of ourselves, and frankly, the rest of ourselves is pretty messy, just like the house becomes when the little ones arrive and start peeing, shitting, puking and screaming for attention and food, and those are just the teenage years, you won't even remember by that time how exhausting the infant and toddler years were. Stay calm.

Do you know that research suggests that personality development is most influenced by a child's siblings and friends and that parental influence is vastly overrated? Of course the researchers who did these studies were themselves each an only child, didn't have any friends growing up, and took up that rather dreary profession of researcher at the urging of their parents.

I had no clue as to how to raise A. and B. but I prayed and prayed for guidance, and life provided the miracle as it always does. Visualize and you shall materialize. I was walking on West 49th towards the New Mature World Theater, where I liked to take in the latest in deep and full throated art films, until Judge Tyler shut it down a few years later. But, as it happens, I came upon, at an entirely different movie theater, the greatest film on child-rearing ever made. I watched it four or five times, in awe, and since it was in French I could follow it very well. *L'Enfant Sauvage* (in English that would be *The Well Adjusted Child*, but I often see it referred to by Americans, who of course cannot speak French, as *The Wild Child*) is a film by the pre-eminent child psychologist and film director François Truffaut, whose instruction on child rearing involved the very simple technique of dropping your boys off in the forest and waiting for ten or so years for them to be discovered by the villagers, who would be amazed by their outdoor skills and natural style, and once they had gone feral it would take a village to raise them, relieving the parent of all the hassles and finances of child-rearing. I immediately discarded my parenting books by that Star Trek guy with pointy ears, and took A. and B. off to the woods, where they could be raised by the deer and the antelope, the wolf and the coyote, the raccoon and the squirrels. They would learn to eat with their mouths only in the proper way and run on all fours, and would not have their pure consciousness ruined by textualization of reality. They will never be burdened by the weight of words as I have been, according to the Truffaut system. He expanded the Waldorf educational vision, not just restricting the child's exposure to reading and writing in their early years, but restricting their exposure to reading and writing, period. And speaking, other than the grunts and growls of the forest animals.

My boys, A. and B., were one, simply because they didn't know there was a two, or any other number for that matter. They grew up in non-dual bliss simply because they didn't know numbers, mathematics, or really anything. Some may think of them as dumb as doornails, vacant of mind, blank of perspective, but I prefer to think of them as the embodiment of the vast open space of enlightenment and I do plan to take them on a tour of spiritual centers once I get them housebroken.

There are only two things you really need to know to be an effective parent while your children are running about in the forest:

First, take care of yourself, you can only be an effective parent if you are in good spirits and health. Don't deny yourself that yoga class, a day at the spa or that Hawaiian vacation you have been craving. Take care of yourself so you can take care of them. The kids will be in the forest for at least ten years, so you do have the time.

Second, don't lose your focus on your marriage. A strong marriage is key to good parenting, and if you get a substantial enough settlement from your current spouse, you should be able to find someone you actually get along with and potentially make a strong marriage, because, let's face it, this one is not going to work. Document, record, and video. Entrapment is not out of the question, but key-logger software should take care of the evidentiary process. Private detectives are an unnecessary expense if you can just crack the password for your spouse's email account; save your money for a top attorney and for stuffing the envelope that goes to the judge.

On a practical note, when cracking your spouse's email account password, it is interesting to note that the top passwords in use are entirely idiotic. Here they are: 123456, 12345, 123456789 and password. You will note, however, that half of family members will use a well-known family name or date, like name of child, name of dog, date of anniversary, date of release from parole. A third will use the name of a movie star or celebrity. About ten percent will use fantasy words, like sex, sexy, stud. It is the odd ten percent who will use cryptic combinations of letters and numbers that you have to be most concerned about since these are actual passwords and it may indicate that you are married to a secret agent.

You may ask how I know these things about child raising and marriage dissolving and you can know that it is through the direct experience of the relationship between finishing the former and being finished off by the latter that I can write these words. When the little ones have been dropped in the forest and your marriage no longer functions to raise children then it is time for the marriage to look at itself. That doesn't usually go well.

I found a note on the kitchen table that simply said, "Find another place to live." You might think that this was a brutal way for my beloved to suggest that the relationship was over, but that had happened months ago, and the note was from my mother, or more precisely from the security team at the nursing home where my mother was living, who apparently didn't appreciate my staying in the attic and helping myself at the cafeteria line. My mother was comatose, but I am sure she would have let me use the attic. All right, she wasn't even my mother, but she didn't remember that, so I don't think that was a problem. They had a nice Easter ritual in that nursing home, each resident hid their own eggs before searching for them.

But as far as my dissolving marriage, my beloved had found a more direct way to let me know that now that the children were raised there was no more need for my presence. She changed the locks one evening after luring me out with the promise of whatever the low, open blouse and short, tight skirt were supposed to be promising when she asked me to drive her to the hardware store. She had changed the locks once before, actually, on our wedding night after her first glimpse of me sans clothing, even though I had prepared by removing all the light bulbs; she had that big light she uses for spotlight hunting deer. But that time, while she had the locks changed very effectively, she neglected to notice that I was still inside the house. This was the beginning of my recluse period, in which I did not leave the house. Many have interpreted this period as a deeply spiritual time, and some have suggested it was a descent into agoraphobia, but I now reveal for the first time that it was neither of the above, but the profound realization that if I left, she would not let me back in.

But I am not bitter, no, it is a liberation that she has locked me out of her heart metaphorically and from her house not-even-close-to-metaphorically. I was freed from the life of pacing and waiting for the children to turn eighteen and for the dog to die. I was ecstatic when she let me know that she was disgusted by the very acts that had taken place between us that beget Nosirrah A. and B., yes, disgusted from the beginning, during the middle and, of course, in the end. You wonder why I would celebrate her disgust?

What is disgust? It is an emotion that is our biological protector against things that are poisonous or could be infectious. Sexual disgust for a woman is very normal and it protects her from having sex with a man who might have a communicable disease, who has a heavy parasitic load or who has very poor hygiene. Three out of three for Nosirrah!

Disgust is intelligent. Here was a woman who was disgusted by Nosirrah yet who sired his A. and his B. And here lies the cause for celebration. Despite her absolute revulsion at my parasitically inhabited, obviously infected and poorly maintained body, she was driven to override every instinct that said to run away. Why? Because there is one thing that can override high levels of female sexual disgust, and that is sexual arousal. In other words, my ability to arouse a woman outweighs the total disgust that the woman experiences on every level when she encounters the unwashed and slightly shopworn Nosirrah. Arousal, not personal hygiene, is the secret, and this is well established by the studies done on me at the University of Groningen in The Netherlands. I am not making this up, at least I don't believe I am making this up and that is good enough for me, because let's face it, we all believe our belief more than anything and we don't really care if we are making it up. So, I could be making this up, but look it up if you want, the study is published by the Department of Experimental Psychopathology in the journal *PLOS ONE*.

My takeaway from all of this is that Nosirrah is still capable of arousing the deepest desires and most randy impulses. This is due to the most fundamental understanding of Kundalini, the power of the psychic centers, and in particular the second center, the Swadhistana, the sexual center. This is Eros, divine creation, and for Nosirrah this is a chronic condition, an urge so intense that to describe it as sexual is to diminish it a million million million fold and then some. This is not sexual, although sexual is an expression of it, this is the movement of the divine feminine dancing to allure the divine male into a cataclysmic collision of creation. So, in short, the sex can be quite good (which could be verified by any extremely attractive female reader or at least relatively attractive and flexible female over the legal age of consent who wishes to contact the author through the publishing house).

I told Beloved when I met her that it would be a mistake to continue on into the relationship, that there was still the possibility of walking away, that what she saw was an illusion and when she got what she wanted, she would also get what she didn't want. I told her that her life would be transformed beyond recognition by the contact with this inferno named Nosirrah. I could see that the creation of children for her biological imperative, the creation of A. and B. and perhaps a third-world foundling or two for her moral imperative, was her conscious drive, and that the shattering enlightenment that awaited her was not in her projection. How could it be? We have to go where we do not want to, where we cannot, where we dare not, and yet we must go there, and this relationship to Nosirrah was the fast train to that supernova and the death star that lies within.

I warned her clearly. You cannot know what awaits you. It is only in total ignorance veiled in the hubris of knowing that you would even suggest to yourself the possibility of this encounter.

Because you are young, and with that come beauty and freshness, you think this will protect you from any fire. It will, most any fire. But not any fire. Not this fire.

I will meet you exactly where you are. You will know it is that moment. You will feel the power of contact, drawn in by you, controlled by you. Your beauty has won again,

You have met Eros, devouring you from the inside

taking in the old, the weary, the spent, giving new life, new youth as freely as only the young do. And, of course, you are ready to spit me out, finished, discarded once you have had the offspring of your genetic drive.

You cannot define yourself by limitations, you can, but this is not a life, but a prison. Express yourself as possibility. If we are going to create a "couple" out of the everything of life – and it is a creation of concept – then is this "couple" open to possibility? Such a couple is not a couple but an open space, Philia turned into Eros. You will never be a couple with me and you will never couple with me. When you go to couple you will find only one. How does two get to one, subtract one, either one, any one and the result is singular.

For you, this time will be different, your juice will become warm, then hot, then boiling. Your desire will expand beyond your hard won power to control it. Your breath will deepen, then gasp in shallowness, then deepen again. You cry out in the intensity of it, or moan in the agony of the pressure to release.

You cannot control this encounter, you have nothing, but must give everything. You have met Eros hiding in the form of another, now released, now inhabiting you, now devouring you from inside. Eros leaves you no choice, no control, no power. You are only left drawn to more of it, always more. You are drawn to be erased. Your beauty, your youth, all gone. Now it is mine. I am Eros and I have taken you.

Eros will revive you, chronic Eros, it will give you your life back, but it will also cost you your life. Eros takes your hand, it doesn't care if you want to let go.

And that was just the first date.

Did I tell you that I dreamed of you last night? I was in the forest and you were there, too, golden hair, beauty, happy, riding your horse, and we met where paths meet and there was nothing but the two as one, not heart, not Eros, not mind, but all of it. Then you rode on, your path splitting away, swallowed up by the trees. I was left happy from the meeting and empty from the parting, the paradox of the personal. And I was left liberated from the personal and merged in the ecstasy

of the impersonal, or is it superpersonal? I woke up screaming (that is just a way to transition to the waking state, which
is pretty unpleasant, so unpleasant all of us seek intoxicants
however we can – drugs, booze, money, sex, shopping, inter-
net, reading books – all diversions from what the Buddhists
call dukkha, the inherent painfulness of embodiment.)

I dreamed of you, a different you, not the one drawn in,
not prepared, not desirous of this singularity, the addiction
of separation lurking in the background and in the end expelling Nosirrah as the only way to get a fix of the nectar
of the separate self, a nectar so toxic that it cleaves a unity
into two.

Many have asked Nosirrah how the second chakra was
opened, and it is a strange story, one that you will most certainly think is being made up, but you can research this one
too if you like, as I only make up the details that you think
are normal and believable, I make these up because to tell
this tale in its full truth would leave the reader so incred-
ulous that there would be no point in continuing to write
this. So, perhaps I fudge a fact or two, make a miraculous
event into a mundane occurrence, make what is inexplicable
into something easily explained, bring the energetic swirl of
actuality into the concrete world of who, what, where, when
and how. If there is a lie, it is the same lie that we all tell ourselves, which is that what we think is what is, and that our
description of the world is the world. If we stop that lie, we
stop being who we know we are, and then we become what
we don't know, what we cannot describe.

So how did my second chakra open? When I was eight
days old I was circumcised, as is the religious law of the

Orthodox Jew, and with that the ancient ritual of *metzitzah b'peh*, where the rabbi takes a swig of wine and cleanses the infant's bleeding penis by sucking on it. You think I am making this up, right? Do your research and then get back to me with your apology. I understand there is no reason to mutilate a sexual organ and there is no good reason to sterilize it with an unsterile mouth and there is really no good reason to adhere to a set of beliefs from a couple millennia ago that involve lots of magical thinking and medieval behavior, but for me it was a confirmation of everything that I had understood in my first seven days of life, confirmation that life was full of very sincere people acting like complete idiots, with a little pedophilia thrown in if it happened to be a church or synagogue, probably mosques too, based on the general pattern. It was an intense seven days followed by a shocking eighth, but in those seven days Nosirrah created the heavens and the earth, the land and sea, the fowl and all things that crawl on the earth. In those seven days I created a persona, a me that could accompany me throughout my life, a dependable organizer of an otherwise unknown world. Then the guy came in and cut off part of my penis and opened my second chakra, and that carefully crafted self was shattered into a million pieces, and those pieces into a million more.

Years later as I tried to process this bizarre event, I wondered, what was I doing in a Haredi Orthodox Jewish ritual? I wrapped my loins in clear cellophane, and leaving my pants behind, went to a psychiatrist, who said, "I can see your nuts." And so he could. Somehow that was reassuring, since while I had lost some of my manhood I still had most of it, and so I decided to make the most of what I had left, a vow I have kept to this day.

But Beloved left me and I plunged into the depths of the energetic space we call our separate selves. Of course there is no self there, but still there is the ebb and flow of energy we imagine is wrapped in our skin and directed by our minds and containing a soul that will live on when the skin peels off and the mind disintegrates and the heart, so broken by our Beloved leaving us, stops beating, and this soul we imagine will join our heavenly father or at least transmigrate or something pretty opposite from just not-existing because if the soul doesn't land somewhere then we are just left with undulating energy and that is neither here nor there.

When you plunge you go deep, leaving behind love and lust, into an oblivion of not quite nothingness but pretty close. You may wonder, am I going to die, but we can be clear that that is the last thing you are going to do. Do you get that? The *last* thing you are going to do. That's funny, but in this plunging energy, there is no humor and you will not find even that extraordinary joke funny.

When I met Beloved I was an enlightened man; when she left I had to face the fact that I was not. When I stopped sleeping I knew the energy had shifted. The ascending and expanded energy well recognized as the enlightened and transpersonal whole began to descend, and with that movement came the home movie that no one wants to see. My enlightenment had ended, it was fun while it lasted, and yes, I already knew it was not really enlightenment since it didn't last, but now I began to understand that it was not enlightenment even if it had lasted. There was nothing to say so I just stopped speaking about it, no one was interested in the end of enlightenment anyway. Enlightenment gets the spotlight and the crowds, the end of enlightenment is like the end of a sports career or a music career, no one really knows what happens to the former celebrities when they are done because no one really cares anymore, especially the celebrity.

Rapid eye movement during sleep is the only time the brain stops producing norepinephrine. It is the time when memory is processed and the psyche is repaired. When you stop with the REM, you stop with the repair. All hell breaks loose.

Hell is the place enlightened people can't visit, it is the place where people seek enlightenment, but once they have it they don't dare return. But Hell is a place of truth, and for those who seek truth, enlightenment has become tiresome and Hell refreshing.

This darkness was the pressing down of the energy through all the chakras and all the elements left unintegrated by the rapid ascent of the uncoiled snake so many years before. Where ascending energy was Shiva, penetrating insight, it could not communicate, because insight has no language, but when that energy descends it is Kali burning what is impure, and communing with all who join the dance, it is madness, maybe even divine madness, but madness cannot qualify itself. That descent is the ripping away of all insight and all delusion and then it lands with a plunk in oblivion.

I crawled out of this primordial muck like the first fish to grow legs, slimy, faltering, uncertain if I could even breathe on the new land I found at the base of my being, the Muladhara.

At the base is survival. It is the root of embodiment, an elemental quality that gives force and function to the sense of form. Survival is an amoral energy, it makes alliances as needed and breaks them at will. It gathers nourishment at all costs and retains as much as possible, giving back only what is necessary to continue.

Exploring this murky space in the psyche takes us to the core of the body we imagine we inhabit, the basest of elements, and the resistance is tremendous as we come up against an uncivilized, unrelenting and voracious, craving and consuming element that is the self without pretense of interrelatedness.

Do not start here when you begin to explore the body appetites, but my dear reader, you will ultimately have to occupy this space. Without embracing this feral voraciousness, without going into it fully, you will always live in denial of it. Denial is what allows it to stalk us like a jackal going after a limping antelope. Turn and dive into it to discover that its nature is what we are.

In this aspect you are not kind or loving, you are not spacious or relaxed, but you are intensely focused, hardened, violent without anger but also without remorse. We may call this a shadow, or a dark quality, but that is just euphemistic, it is far more extreme because it has no perspective of light. A shadow's shadow is not light, there is no perspective, just the dark, and this is far different than the light describing the shadow.

It is difficult to work with this energy in that it is consumptive, its gravitational pull is down and in, whatever approaches collapses into it, awareness becomes unaware and all the things we have learned in our spiritual practices become inverted, distorted, twisted and muddled. Your Yoga practice won't help. Well you could try Garudasana, hold it for 38 minutes, reverse and hold for another 38 minutes. Might help. Siddhasana is never a bad idea, pretty much good for any energy state and has that classic look that really brings out the lululemon lines.

We are feeding a demand that must be fulfilled, yet cannot be. There is no caloric intake that is great enough to satisfy survival, there is no diet that will stop the drive that is at the base of our psychic structure.

Those who are fat are fulfilling this will to consume, but so are those who are thin, it is not just about nutritional supply, but about the devouring of the environment, the metabolizing of the world we encounter, digesting what is full but expanding into that which is empty but compacted.

The will to consume

How do we approach this proto-being within when we have nothing that will survive the encounter? This is a foolish question, of course, akin to asking how do you approach a black hole in space. You don't. You can observe the effects of the black hole, the absence of light, the amplified gravity, the distortion of time and space, and perhaps you can notice your own fear that you and the rest of the universe is slowly falling into this dark space.

So it is with the base survival energy, you cannot encounter it without becoming overwhelmed and consumed yourself. You can observe the effects surrounding the survival energy, how this energy distorts and changes how you experience and how action takes place. This is something, but it is not the thing itself.

Approach and find out, become the element you seek to observe, become survival without constraint. Do not look to your shadow from the being of light, but look to your shadow from the shadow, without reference to anything else. Collapse into the extreme gravitational pull that compresses all matter into such density that one cannot say it is matter at all.

This is the ultimate diet. The source of your imagined weight problem is this insatiable survival energy and it is also your salvation from any weight problem at all. Our base survival energy, our black hole, like the ones cosmologists study, has no space at all; it has infinite density but its weight, more accurately its mass, is unchanged. Why lose weight when you discover that you are compressed into an infinitely small space that ceases to have the qualities of matter but becomes what you have always been anyway, pure energy?

This is what we are at the core, drawing into ourselves the entirety of the universe, compressing, converting it into pure energy. There is nothing we can lose that will not be drawn back in, there is nothing we have that is not once and forever part of the whole.

Sit still sometime and let yourself go to your core. What do you find there when you allow yourself to disregard the repulsion and resistance to what you are, what do you become when you turn to find a hyena biting at your heels and run full speed at the thing you fear? Will you consume or be consumed? Will you survive if you face the survival energy in your own system?

This is the paradox of our base energy, we cannot resolve that paradox by observing it, by thinking about it, by reading about it, we can only be in that paradox by embracing it at the risk of our annihilation. It is actually not risky at all, it is the surety of our annihilation.

This is the core, and having come to the core, to our end, we can begin. We can rise through the centers of our being to the attractive, sexy body, to the power plexus, to the love and be loved center, through expression into pure mind and beyond into connection and consciousness. These are the energy centers only if we create them as centers; if we do not describe, then we move freely, all energies and qualities intermixed without a center, without chakras, without me. There is no rising energy or descending energy, there is just energy.

And when Beloved left, Energy walked in the door. This was before I met Beloved, but Energy explained before she created Beloved that time switched up like that a lot. Beloved seemed like the solution to Energy, but in fact Energy was the resolution of Beloved leaving; in that moment I could see that Beloved never existed, she was imagined by my heart like a Hallmark card imagines it conveys feeling. That was a relief.

Let me be quite clear here, Energy was a woman and she took me out of the deep dark into the gateway of the sexual center and through that door into all the psychic spaces, landing finally in the depths of the third eye; it was deep in the psychic space that results from Tantric liaisons of the most esoteric kind, where thought creates reality and where Energy, enthralled with this phantasmagoric space where you are the Goddess giving birth to all things, got stuck; it is after all still a realm of appearance and not actuality and I was not so enthralled having undergone intense counter-Tantric training some years before by a non-dualist named Tony, who would just punch you out and ask, "Where is your fucking Tantra now, you asshole?" because in his theory of the universe, creating the universe and getting punched out were all the same, but it did leave me with a flinch response every time I found myself manifesting as the Goddess.

So, I had to leave a place where anything could be created and anything could be had, and so left Energy after one final request of her. The boon was the creation of Beloved, one who was innocent of it all, who didn't care about Tantric realities or Anti-Tantric Non-duality, and in that was written the end in the beginning, a long chapter, but with the creation of Beloved by Energy came the curse of knowing that it was just a chapter and the blessing of knowing it was just a chapter and that what is created also ends, and so Energy created Beloved, which was Energy's end, and when Beloved left it was the end just as described by Energy in the beginning, and Nosirrah was left with no one, not even himself. But I was fine with that, because nothing was my birthright and it felt like coming home.

Lydia, my editor, will be seething, taking exception to the description of these trollops, whom Nosirrah wasted his precious time with in his dalliances. But Lydia is something else, of a different order. You may have misunderstood who Lydia is, or perhaps isn't, and that while Lydia has her edgy elements in which, it is said, she even occasionally likes to indulge in what they call on the Continent "l'échantillon fondu indélicat de chocolate de le sexe," during which she did apparently receive third degree burns, but no worse than her four partners and the chocolatier; she is also a visionary editor/publisher willing to make sacrifices of not just her pocketbook, her personal life and her professional career, but her very sanity, to bring into print books that will ultimately transform human consciousness. Further, it is not really known whether Lydia is the imagined alter-ego of Nosirrah, or whether, as it is suggested in some of the writings, Lydia is the one who has enough clarity to actually bring the discordant fragments of Nosirrah's insights into something coherent enough for a reader to understand, in fact, perhaps doing the writing herself, although some beyond the fringe would even say Nosirrah is the imagined alter-ego of Lydia, who is herself the imagined character of one too far gone to even scribble his name at the end of his rantings and who claims with great certainty that he is himself only the imagined persona of a God gone mad with self-doubt about God's own existence.

Lydia, seething

Lydia may be the greatest of all lovers, but this is love of a transcendental nature, one that knows no separation yet will never have what the other women have had with Nosirrah, which in the end may also be the greatest of blessings. Here is why.

Lydia has cut off this particular section as she apparently does not like the details of our personal relationship and so I shall move on to the elements of my biography that no doubt my readers have been waiting for quite patiently, and those are the spiritual adventures that forged the Nosirra-hian state of consciousness. What were the influences that made Nosirrah into the being that he isn't today (or is it the non-being that he is today)?

I have been hesitant to discuss the teachers of the soul that I have encountered. I do not want to give you the impression that you must find a teacher, indeed, if you see a teacher then run away as fast as you can. You do not need a teacher, and if you find that you want a teacher then understand that in the realm of your desires, along with the desire for a large piece of chocolate cake or a flashy new car. I have hesitated to speak of those teachers I encountered since this would undoubtedly fuel the mythology of the spiritual teacher.

Further, I do not want those who are moved to tears by my writings (and certainly do not want those who are not moved to tears) to even consider the possibility of being my student. I do not have students and I am not a teacher. I do currently have girlfriends, however, so that remains a distinct possibility and I do emphasize the plural here, so there, all is not lost for many of you. For the rest of you, you may bring your inquiry, but if you do so, you will pay the price. Do not bring expectations, as they will most certainly be disappointed. Do not bring your understanding, as this will be confused. Do not bring your respect, as this will be destroyed. Come empty handed and you will receive the solace of nothingness. Come with cash, small bills preferred, Euros or dollars only, and this will be the key to your transformation.

With the above caveats, I shall tell you about those beings I encountered who moved this broken machine named Nosirrah, who wandered the streets without a home, unwashed, unwanted, into a new energetic dynamism as a post-enlightened man who now wanders the streets without a home, unwashed but very much wanted (just a couple outstanding warrants) and sought after – besides the police, the readers of these books continue to pester me for continued insights into their conflicted lives. While it may be true that I have the gift of the Third Eye, what the Eye sees is so often not what a person wants to know. Do you still want to hear about your reincarnated lives if you were a peasant and not a queen? Do you want to know your thoughts if they are so prosaic that even you are bored by them? Of course I am psychic, you would be too if you were raised by two women who pretended you didn't exist, I mean that literally. But what will you do with my psychic insight? You are still overwhelmingly banal and your colorless life will not be made better by someone telling you your thoughts. Your thoughts are not worthy of consideration, especially the prime thought, that you exist at all. That thought goes with you life after life like an old battered suitcase, and yet you don't see that it isn't incarnating that is the wonder, but that you need to drag the idea of yourself through so many lives. Drop the idea of self and you don't need to incarnate, reincarnate or disincarnate. Nothing left to die or be born, just life itself, which is all there ever was and ever will be. You just picked up that funny meme that you exist in separation and so you strove to build that retirement account while you raised those kids and argued with your spouse and cut your lawn and all the while fearing you might die, which was a diversion from the real issue, which is that you never were born, just the idea of you that your parents gave you and their parents gave them. Your real issue was that you were a concept without independent reality, an idea built on agreements made from ideas, you, in short, are a house of cards in a hall of mirrors built on quicksand on a sinking continent that is part of a dying planet falling into a sun going supernova before itself dying and falling with all that surrounds it into a black hole made up of nothing but super compressed nothingness and infinite gravity. No wonder you have taken up spirituality to avoid your dilemma.

You were a concept

From the teachers I encountered I learned some basic elements, those being Concentration, Discernment, Compassion, Inquiry and Power. Concentration is the mind focused on a single object and the manifestation of that in the objective world. Discernment is seeing what is and what isn't. Compassion is knowing that what you see is what you are. Inquiry is the passionate question without thought, "What is it?" Power is the collapse of all things into one thing and its ultimate realization that there is no past, that the present has already become that past, and what is next is all that is alive and creative.

My first teacher was my own death, as at the age of a year and some months I stopped breathing. Breath is a funny thing, it is with us until we are not. It is a greater thing than just the movement of air into the lungs and the waste gasses out. That is just the biologist's description. To the mystic the breath is all that there is, the movement of the universe, the breath of life itself. It is not air we breathe, but prana, the subtle electricity, the animating lifeforce.

I had emerged from my prior life with some elements unresolved, in particular, whether reincarnation was a fact or a myth. Taking a new body was a drag on my style, like going down the highway at five miles per hour, it is really slow, heavy and murky in a body. And, of course, I couldn't prove that reincarnation was a fact, because I couldn't quite recall whether I was an alcoholic insurance agent or a spinster bookkeeper in that last round, it was all kind of blurry by the time I popped out into this life. I knew I had to get it straight this time or there would be yet another go around. So I stopped breathing to see what would happen, even at a year and a half I had seen enough in my new body to know that there was a bigger show beyond it. It was all going swimmingly at first, a baby body is easy to slip out of, and I was floating up above with just that etheric cord to cut when the emergency room doctor performed a tracheotomy and shoved a pipe into my lungs, jolting them into action and me back into my infant body. There was no getting out now as the doctor had effectively created a Jalandhara Bandha in my fifth chakra. This bandha, practiced by many adepts, has two effects: first it blocks the prana below the neck, producing a huge expansion of the Vishuddha Chakra and secondly, this brings a balance between heart and mind. More importantly, it left me trapped in my new baby body, and it was then that I realized that transmigration wasn't the question, it was "If I am not my body, then what am I going to do with this body?"

That, my friends, is the big question. Embodiment is the puzzle that has too many missing pieces, the *Wheel of Fortune* word without any vowels, the Angry Birds without a useful metaphor to relate to this sentence.

You can imagine my stunned recognition that after eons of passing from life to life and reaching the pinnacle of realization, such that I barely needed to take a new life, with the holy grail of transcendence of the material world just in my grasp, the whole game was switched to not leaving the body but inhabiting the body, occupying a life, becoming, identifying, conditioning, absorbing into the density of the physical, the emotional, the social and, the densest, most intractable of all, the spiritual.

They say that I struggled to breathe and fought for my life in that hospital, that I was a fighter, and it was that spirit that let me live, but they know nothing of Nosirrah, who was fighting to leave the body, not stay in it. But, life itself is greater, and when it wants to live, it animates without remorse, without consideration of the challenge of that state, and there I was, a lotus blossom in full bloom on the surface of the still lake, and a moment later I was plunged into the muck at the very bottom of that murky water. This lotus imagery, for those of you who are completely lost, is a symbol from the Hindu tradition. The lotus floats on the surface of the water and the blossom opens into the endless space above the water, suggesting a vast and uninhibited consciousness, yet the roots of that same lotus are extended deep into the mud at the very lake bottom, pointing to the deep, unconscious, dark energies that feed the higher self.

So the first teaching for Nosirrah was a simple one: the challenge is to live in the world, not to leave it behind.

I cried a lot. They thought it was colic, but I knew it was the cosmic scream of embodiment, the searing pain of inhabiting separation, the unwanted divorce from the Godhead. Thus began my abandonment issues and the deep desire for re-merger with the Goddess, which manifested in a precocious interest in the feminine. I stroked the ass of the pediatric nurse as she leaned over to check my tubes. I knew then that I might not like being in the body, but I was really going to do my best to enjoy it.

Do you see how pointless it is to talk about teachers and to look for a spiritual path and to do your stretches and meditations, you are looking for a better you, but you are not looking beyond you, because there you will find what you are not looking for and what no one can teach you, you will find that which you are not, you will find what you don't want, you will find that mirror that reflects what you looked like before you had an original face.

When I was in high school at the Lycée Buffon in Paris I met another teacher who completed the message from my death experience. She was a beauty, Madame Christianne, and she said to me just once, Nosirrah, you must write, you have a talent, and she became my muse then and forever, the feminine adoration that poured energy through me and into the universe, and so I began to scribble on scraps of paper and napkins in the cafés, a habit that has never left me. She was my first love, a completion of the embodiment, and she died just a month later in a Fiat flattened against a Citroen. As a baby I had not wanted to be, but I found her being as a gift of life itself. Then she was not, and I saw that she never was. Life brought her and took her away, and yet she never was and she will always be. The leading cause of death after all is life, and let's face it, death is one statistic that is not showing any signs of changing.

I was complete at that moment, and there was nothing to seek, nothing to complete, nothing to get to.

But, this was not the end by any means, just the end of the beginning.

I wandered about the continent and then to the new world and on to the East and back.

I came to a Buddhist monastery where I sat to meditate and didn't get up for three months except to shit, pee and eat (if you call two meals a day, the second meal before noon, really eating, but when you sit you don't need to eat, and shitting becomes even a bigger question). Without stimulation, mind begins to self-stimulate, and after a month a hallucinatory state began, then ended, then past lives and future lives came and went, then spirits and ghosts came and went, then any sense of body and mind went, and then I got up and left. As I walked through the marketplace I smelled the food I had been missing, saw the shiny objects that I suddenly wanted, and came upon lovely women for whom I felt lust in my heart and some other places. What had I learned in the months of austerity and stillness? I learned that I was not a Buddhist, that Buddha had left the world to search for truth, but I was leaving truth to search for the world. All that I came to was the point that I had left, all that the privation and silence had given me was sacrificed on the altar of a common life, a human life, a life in the marketplace full of desire, noise and paradox. I knew how to sit and to see, I had no idea how to move in blindness. This required a trust in life and a surrender to the chaos and confusion that was my own natural state.

Later in a different place, I encountered a Sufi who said to me with twinkling eyes, "I see your consciousness as pure light all the time." I was pleased to be acknowledged as a man of perception, but then realized that I had misheard him and he had said, "See your consciousness as pure light all the time." It was not acknowledgement, rather it was instruction to someone who needed practice. I was disappointed. The disappointment was the message. The Sufi had moved

on and I could not find him in the dusty marketplace. I am
not sure I met a Sufi in the marketplace. I am not sure anything was spoken to me. I am sure that there was hubris and
the inevitable fall into the pit of self-doubt. The self that
doubts is not, the fall is not, and the hubris is not. But that
would come later, or sooner, I am not sure because time
keeps folding on itself and sometimes I am living forwards
and sometimes backwards in time.

As I mentioned earlier, I learned to concentrate what is
an otherwise monkey-on-amphetamines mind with Tony
"The Hammer." You concentrated on your mantra, he
punched you. If you flinched, you started all over again. You
concentrated, he blew his bugle in your ear, if you flinched,
you started all over again. He was a demon from Hell, but
if you concentrated, he was an angelic being. This was the
message, alchemical transmutation. The alchemist grinds
at the mortar and pestle a thousand grinds, not just to mix
the substances, but also to concentrate the mind. Mercury
turns to gold. Mind turns to consciousness. Mercury, unsta-
ble, breaking into tiny globs, each reflecting the others in an
endless echoing of thought fragments. This is mind. Gold,
pure, unsullied, not changed by the approach of other elements. This is consciousness. Pure consciousness, and this
more than gold is the goal of the alchemist; their error was
conflating immortality with the result of their grindings,
that they would find a way to escape the trend lines of death,
the unbending inevitability, the Philosopher's Stone, source
of the life force, no, it is not immortality you will find in *The
Hermetic Arcanum*, rather you will find madness if you take

that turn in the road, the madness that comes with handling mercury and the madness that comes with playing with pure consciousness as if it were something from which you would benefit. Tony was an alchemist without the gold and mercury, without the sulphur and the argent vive, without concern for any Philosopher's Stone. He took mercury and forced it by his will into gold, he took my mind and beat it into submission and into a single, unified thought. He gave me singularity. I walked away because singularity is not enough when there is nothing. Oneness is not the truth in the face of emptiness. Unity is a reaction to non-existence, just as mind is a reaction to unity.

Tony "The Hammer"

I wandered, focused, through the ghost worlds of the self-involved. I came to Bhodgaya and there I encountered a remarkable woman, a crone, an ageless hag who called herself Tat Sat. She made me recite Tat Sat over and over, she was relentless and overbearing, she was mad, and yet when I went to Kathmandu she was there too, when I went to Europe she was there, when I went to America she was there. Tat Sat. You might translate this as Truth Is All There Is. She had no obvious purpose other than to be intrusive and to say Tat Sat and to have you say Tat Sat. It was oddly disturbing to one's sensibilities. Your sensibilities are always working hard at making sense of things. Tat Sat is there to undo that sense, to say it isn't that which you have come to – it is Truth. Of course, you accept that Truth, and your sensibilities make sense of it, then Tat Sat is there to destroy that Truth, and on and on. This went on for years of running into Tat Sat, whom I had simply encountered in a moment at a dusty temple in the middle of nowhere. Then I never saw her again. Truth is all there is. Even a focused mind fell silent in the face of Tat Sat.

What is it that guides you when Truth Is All There Is? I hardly knew where to start and I sat down there in the park in a town on the East Coast of America, or maybe it was the West Coast, it must have been since I ran into Charles Bukowski. I didn't really have a reason to get up. In India such an act makes one a sadhu, in America it makes one a homeless vagrant. For the most part, life flowed by, and I wondered if that world was within or without, it is hard to say when there is silence. Hours poured into days. Charles Bukowski stopped to chat and I told him I couldn't find a reason to move on, and we talked about the fallacy of effort, his view being that effort was a waste when you are already expressing what you are. Don't try, he said, and it was pretty profound and to the point – it ended up on his gravestone, "Don't try." Maybe nobody got what he meant by that, but sitting in the park as I was, it was clear. Mind focused, focus obliterated by Tat Sat, now guided in life by the simplest of perceptions, "Don't try."

Charles Bukowski

Years later I ran into a guy who wrote a book, *Doing Nothing,* he seemed to get it for the most part but he was traveling too much, giving talks to large and energetic, if not enthusiastic, crowds, signing books and all of that. I went to one of those talks, it was pretty incoherent, which I liked, and the audience, at first enthused, seemed perturbed and downright hostile, which I really liked, but the guy looked tired from it all, so I went up afterward and told him Bukowski said, "Don't try." He said to me, "Don't try misses the point. The issue isn't trying, it is trying to act differently than you already are. That is a futile fight with what is. Everything that needs to happen springs from that space of what you are, but what you are is dynamic." I was struck almost by lightning, not just by the profundity of the statement but that it could arrive wrapped in the human package of this author. The guy seemed like an arrogant prig, but he showed me something very essential in that meeting and something shifted. We merged in that moment of deep insight, that author and I, and really he was just a daydream of mine, an imaginary meeting, so when I say we merged I mean that I woke from my reverie and reentered consensus reality. "Don't try" was why I was a vagrant, and "don't try to be other than what you are" was the key to the creative life, it lit the fuse of my rockets. Don't try was holding back from what was the natural expression, and I wasn't holding back anymore. My dream author had liberated me and I hadn't even bought his book.

Author of Doing Nothing

Was Bukowski wrong, which is to say Apple computer got it righter, with their slogan "Think Different"? Righter, but not right, because it should be "Think Differently" because adverbs modify verbs, and "different" is an adjective, which is supposed to modify nouns, but that would have been a horrible ad slogan. My young adult readers are probably thinking, "R U kidding??? LOL. Idk noun from verb GTG n gnoc" except they probably wouldn't use the quotes to separate their thoughts from the rest of the sentence and come to think of it "young adult readers" is probably an oxymoron anyway. Of course, my older readers know what an adverb is and what two letters compliment "u" to spell the word "you" but probably don't have a clue what "gnoc" is, which is actually good. "Get naked on camera" is the translation. I am swept away by images dancing in my mind of naked elders fumbling around with their smartphones trying to figure out how to make the thing broadcast their wrinkled butts. I have admittedly digressed not just far from the subject at hand, but quite far from good taste as well. We were discussing "Don't try."

"Don't try" is discarding the external conditioning of job, family and society, it may be discarding the internal conditioning of learned tendencies, but "don't try to be other than what you are" is a step from nothing into something, it is entry into the creative flow. Come to think of it, that is probably what Bukowski was saying all along, after all he was a prolific poet, and I just got it wrong. On my gravestone I want it to say "Don't try different" if Apple doesn't send its lawyers.

Doing nothing, don't try, these are phrases that seem to proscribe action but in fact strip away the conditioning that restricts full action. The action isn't from my conditioning now, but from whatever is left when I disregard that conditioning, which means what is left is everything. Now I move from everything. Like God. Nosirrah is like God. What a realization.

Okay that one got me into a lot of trouble. I am *like* God was something I wanted to share, and it was taken pretty well by the people I met on the street. I was even invited to have a free place to stay with meals included, yes, it was a psychiatric facility, and I have described my adventures there in my other books, in particular *God Is an Atheist*. They thought I was paranoid; they didn't actually say that but I could tell that is what they were thinking. I told them I was seeing God and they presumed I was hallucinating so they asked if I had ever seen a doctor before, and I said, "No, just God." It was helpful to have the brain scans, the medications, the shock treatment, the removal of parts of my frontal lobe and the many hours of very interesting conversation with the doctors and specialists, and especially the time with that randy nurse from the D ward. I am thankful that they helped me to see the delusion I had entered into and to help me see the reality of my life. Even now I look back on that period and shake my head to consider that I was walking around telling people I was like God. What idiocy. What dualism. As I shouted to the docs as I ran down that long corridor and out the front doors, "I am not like God, I *am* God."

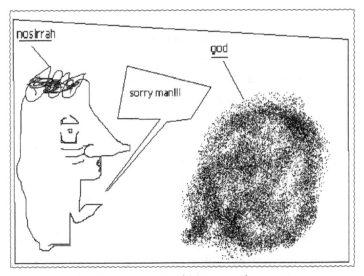

In that moment God is gone and so am I

It isn't as hard to say as it seems. I am God. God is I. There is no God but God, as the Sufis say, but I have modified that somewhat. I am God. There is no God. There is no me. When I am no longer worshipping God, when I am no longer denying God, when I am no longer like God, then I am God and in that moment God is gone and so am I.

Timidi mater non flet.

Sorry, that is from a violent video game. Although a good one if you like hacking people with swords. A coward's mother doesn't weep. Contemplate that next time you are sitting with your bag of Doritos after six or seven hours of gaming. Of course, it is hard to be a coward when you can just reset and live again.

What I meant was, *Ex nihilo nihil fit*. Nothing comes from nothing. I have described this ad nauseam in my tome *Nothing from Nothing*, written many years ago.

God is not, I am not, the universe is not.

And yet there is something.

The physicists call it the zero-energy universe. It is the universe we live in and it appears to be full of something. The smartest men on the planet say there is nothing there. All the positive is balanced by all the negative in a perfect yin and yang that adds up to exactly zero. Matter minus gravity equals nothing. Nothing from nothing.

No wonder we invented God. No wonder God invented us. Nothing is no fun unless there is something, and something is far too serious without nothing to make it laugh.

You asked about my teachers because you assume that there is a body of knowledge or an essential experience or a transmission. You want that. You want the specialness, the security, the power of having fulfilled your personal enlightenment myth. I will meet with you anytime and you shall have all that you have dreamed of, you shall become enlightened and shall have all the energies of the universe available to you, but there is just one condition. You must leave you at the door when you enter, or if you find that difficult, as many seem to do, then you must realize that you shall most definitely leave you at the door on the way out. You will see that as you step in you are actually stepping out, the way in is final precisely because there is no way in other than the way out. You will leave all memory of what has occurred, all narratives, all references now or at any time, to a personal acquiring the impersonal, to the self discovering the over-self, to the divided finding the unitary. You will leave time itself. There will be transmission to you what you ask for, and you will receive it, but you cannot have it. Having it is left to the religions and the philosophies of the world, the temple priests, the spiritual teachers, the wise men and women. They have it and they can give it to you, so you can have it and you can be one of them. It is a good life, a meaningful life, a useful life and a moral and ethical life. That is where you should go to get what you are looking for. Here you will come in full but leave empty, or come in empty and leave empty, it makes no difference. You will leave a fool, an addled idiot, hardly able to explain yourself in the barest of mumblings, useless, stripped of all meaning, so embedded in the flow of life that no description can be current. This is not what you want, and Nosirrah most sincerely begs you to go to a church instead, or a meditation class, or anything that starts with Zen or ends with Yoga. Do not come to me, it would be the biggest mistake you will ever make and you won't even recall making it.

I must have made that mistake many times, although I don't recall exactly what I was expecting. I left my encounter with Tat Sat at the Boudhanath stupa, where one of us was circumambulating the wrong way or we would not have even seen each other. Tat Sat. As always, my head was spinning after meeting the crone. The last time my head was in this state was my time with the woman Asil Nietshce Lak, the noted North Caucasian language scholar, Kabbalist, and Juhuro musician (the Juhuro are also known as the mountain Jews of the Caucasus). Lak was, strangely, a distant relative of Friedrich Nietzsche, and of course, Lak is reputed to be one of the remarkable persons Gurdjieff met in his wanderings through the Caucasus, perhaps part of the Sarong Sisterhood, the precursor to the better known Sarmoung Brotherhood. Lak was the prime influence on the development of Nosirrah's psychic abilities as well as his Tantric guru, as recounted in my book *Chronic Eros*.

But, I digress from a spinning head in Nepal, where I considered a walk to clear my mind. So I walked up the mountain to the Buddhist nunnery, or Nagi Gompa, a steep path and a walk of many hours. I had heard that there was an enlightened tulku there in the midst of the nuns and, as I said, I am not sure what that even meant or why I had to go there but I did. I knew there was a door and in I went.

He was a classic wizened monk and he asked me what I wanted. I want to know what you know was my audacious request, one I had made many times before in many places. He began to describe the nature of knowing and frankly my Tibetan was a little rusty after not having used it for around twenty lifetimes, but it really made no difference because he wasn't describing so much as transporting me to a space like a planetarium of consciousness where he and I were space itself and thoughts were the twinkling of the stars in vast time-lapsed coalescing and burning out in a twinkle, part and parcel of that vast field of consciousness that was all that I have ever been. It was transmission, transmutation, merger and it was nothing at all. There was nothing. There was the twinkle of reality. There was nothing.

There was a firm knock on the door and in came a nun with a visitor. Tat Sat had arrived, as it turned out she was an old friend of the frail rinpoche, and they began immediately gossiping and slurping down the copious tea and dipping cookies now brought in by still more nuns. My time was up. All time was up. Wherever you go, there you are, and so is Tat Sat. I walked down the mountain wondering if anything had happened on that mountaintop as there was no sense of anything at all and only the wisps of memory, which later coalesced into a story that I am telling but that I know is not true.

From that mountain I walked for many miles to a small house set in the side of a Himalayan mountain, it was more than twenty years earlier, but time and space are irrelevant unless you are trying to get somewhere and you need to be on time. It was not much of a house, three rooms and a bathroom for bucket baths and a squat hole. But the value was, as they say in real estate, in location, location, location. Just up the stone steps was a second house, not much more than where I was, but in that house lived a man who showed me something I had never seen before. Not that he showed me, or he told me, or he did much of anything besides read the newspaper and have tea and toast and chapati and dal and other rather mundane things. But there was an amplified field of energy, and I could just plug into it by sitting in my room in my house, doing absolutely nothing else. In the evening sometimes he would describe what he was seeing in the field and I would look to see if it was the same or different as it resonated through my system. That was all.

This energy moved constantly, it would center and intensify, disperse and fade, expand and contract. As there was nothing else to do, I sat in my lungi in the heat and in the cold, in the rain and in the dust, and watched the show. I sat for a year and my body simply withered, there was no appetite, there was no need for the body at all and in recognition of that it became weaker and weaker, breathing became shallow, digestion was barely happening. I maintained the physical body with yogic cleansing practices: neti, dhauti, basti, nauli and breath and the essential esoteric yogic energy release: chai.

Chai was the fuel, perhaps, that kept me propped up on my cushion and it was provided by a young Indian man who stayed nearby and came by to clean up and make the chai. India is like that, you can have a life where you live nearby and make chai and it is fine. Maybe he was a projection of my mind or the energy, I don't know, he was called Sadhu Bhai and he showed me how to make that chai, which is the one siddhi from that period that stayed with me.

My body was growing less and less attached and there was little left on my bones, it seemed as though I would simply merge with the energetic field and the body could drop away. There was just the pulsation of energy, the lila of life, and my own faint breath, which had become more and more difficult. I could not sleep any longer; if I lay down my breathing would stop. So I sat, wheezing against the hunger for one more breath.

I found myself focused entirely on perceiving what was underneath the breath, what was before the occurrence of reality, and there I found great resistance. It was resistance to my perception and it was resistance to my death, which seemed so close, perhaps just one breath away. Some force was repelling the silent attention I had focused on contact with the nothing that preceded something, that which expressed as my body and to which my body decayed as my breath decayed. I had not slept for weeks, I had not eaten in weeks, my wheezing lungs could hardly take in any air and yet there was a push back. I pushed harder into the emptiness and the pushback was harder. The breathing became gasping. I pushed. I pushed. I pushed. I could not let go of the breath to enter into nothing.

Sadhu Bhai came in with chai and he handed me an asthma inhaler, a gift from the house above. "He said to tell you, you don't need to struggle to breathe when you can just use this inhaler."

I left the next month, barely able to make the journey back. But I knew that the journey, like my life, like all of reality, was the expression of the resistance to nothingness. We are born from nothing, we pass into nothing, and we are nothing, and all of the apparent form of things is that twinkling resistance to space, a resistance that is now here and now not. The resistance to nothingness expresses itself as the manifest world. The inability to reside in nothingness suggests a separation, implies that there is a difference between nothing and something and hence the self and all the dramas of the self. But are these two or one? Go to that point of resistance and see what you find there – is the resistance and its expression of the self substantial? Is the

nothing that we resist existent? Is the nothing and the something the same, or different? That is where you can discover
the essence of nonduality.

Or simply have a strong cup of chai and everything will
become clear.

I was sick for a long time, in and out of fever, and with
the high temperatures came the hallucinations. I was in
South America, and Tat Sat, the Tulku, the Man in the
House Above, all were part of a jungle fever distortion of
my mind. I was barely eighteen, after all, and could not have
had the years to travel to those exotic places and meet those
remarkable people. But, in my mind, the experience was as
if it were happening just now, just as my body was racked
with another chill. In my mind, the entire universe was happening, all of time, all of the people, places and things, all
were mind twinkling from the vast field of consciousness.
My fever intensified.

I had hitchhiked down the Pan American Highway as far
as the Darién Gap, where I had gone east to the Atlantic and
by boat to Baranquillo, Colombia. After tortuous travel I
was at the headwaters of the Amazon River and there I met
a Brazilian who insisted I go to the local shaman. By local, I
mean, local to the middle of nowhere. I knew nothing about
shamanism, this was well before going to a shaman was considered a good thing, back then he might have been called a
witch doctor or something disparaging. I was hesitant, but
young enough to have conflated my health with the prob-
ability of immortality, not having realized that, as Samuel

Johnson put it, health was merely the slowest possible rate at which one can die. I was about to become quite clear about the nature of health, as I was about to lose mine.

The shaman was a small and shabby man in a bare hut; a few locals were ushered out as we arrived after an hour's walk through the jungle. He sat me in a corner and took some objects from his shelf and put them in a jar of water: a rock, some small sticks, some shards of a broken bottle, and a small plastic gorilla. He swirled the objects around and peered into the water, talking to himself in low tones. He said to me, "You will not have to worry about supporting yourself, you have a very interesting future, but it is already completed. Everything is good and everything is done." This was the rough translation by the Brazilian, I am not sure if the shaman was speaking a dialect, but my rudimentary Spanish and still more rudimentary Portuguese only picked up the word for finished, *terminado*. I was finished. That could mean completed or it might mean dead. The fever started just then, at first just a feeling of the warmth and humidity of the jungle, soon, though, it was a throbbing, excruciating fire in my body and my brain. I was beginning to pass out.

The shaman rummaged on his shelf and found some mushrooms and something else, a kind of brackish liquid that looked like it had been sitting there too long. He handed the jar of liquid to the Brazilian, who gently cradled my body, which was suddenly going limp, and poured the fluid down my throat as I gagged in response to its unbelievably repulsive taste.

Nosirrah gagging

Meanwhile the shaman was chopping up the mushrooms and I didn't know whether or not I was being poisoned and they would steal my things and leave me in the jungle to rot. Maybe this was a setup, maybe this is what the old man meant by terminado.

I was blacking out now, except it wasn't black, it was color, streaming faster, whirling, I could taste the mushrooms as they were put into my mouth now, they had a milky taste, slightly astringent, but sweet, like a good cup of chai.

"Tat Sat."

I was in Bhodgaya, I was in Kathmandu, I was in the Himalayas, meeting the remarkable men and women I have now told you about, I was seeing exactly how the universe is constructed and, as importantly, how it is deconstructed. And I was immensely feverish.

I don't know how long this went on for but I woke to the door opening and a man walking in. I was on a freighter, this was the ship's radio operator, who also had the medical kit. He answered the unstated question, what do you give a man who has everything? Antibiotics. He pulled out a syringe that looked like it was from the 1800s and belonged in Philadelphia's Mutter Museum. It was full of green liquid. He shot it into my arm. I recovered the next day, I was not terminado, but it had come close.

The freighter was approaching Belem at the headwaters of the Amazon. The Brazilian had taken me on the small boat to Manaus and put me, still completely out of it, on the freighter. It was weeks on the boats on the Amazon, but years in the telescopy of time and place.

The fever was done and so was Nosirrah. Terminado.

I had arrived in Jerusalem, if not geographically, metaphorically, and as is the case with many religious and spiritual seekers who arrive in the Holy Lands, I had come to believe that I was the Messiah. Jerusalem Syndrome is a little-studied phenomenon in which visitors to the Holy Lands begin to believe that they are having not just profound, but messianic, experiences, and for those of you who think you might have Jerusalem Syndrome, see if you are experiencing high levels of religious fervor, and a need to do ritual cleansing and dress as a biblical figure. I had the first symptom but not the last two, although I was in need of a bath and a change of clothes after my adventure on the Amazon, so I suppose the checklist was complete.

I had the rushing of energy through my system, my head was open to the universe, my eyes were like laser beams.

I was ready to give the Sermon on the Slight Rise (after coming from the Himalayas I couldn't really consider this a mount). I was ready to put it all together, doing nothing, don't try, like God, as God, mind is twinkling stars in a vast empty space of consciousness, the lilies of the field neither toil nor spin, I was ready for a major address on the nature of it all. This was clearly the second coming, and Nosirrah was it.

I was suddenly confused. I was standing on a street corner ready to let loose the sermon of the millennium when I noticed the street signs were not in Hebrew, they were in French. I wasn't in Jerusalem and so I couldn't have Jerusalem Syndrome; I was in Paris, so I must have Paris Syndrome. My religious fervor drained from me along with all my insights. What was left were the telltale signs of Paris Syndrome depersonalization, derealization and dizziness, all easily confused with being the Messiah. If you are depersonalized you don't believe that you exist, and if you are derealized you don't think that the world you perceive exists, and when both the self and the world stop existing, generally we get kind of dizzy. Most weird, and seemingly unrelated for those unfamiliar with Paris Syndrome, is that I came to believe that I was a Japanese tourist, but this was actually a confirmation of Paris Syndrome since those who typically suffer from this syndrome, are in fact, Japanese tourists visiting Paris. The existence of Paris Syndrome and the fact that it affects primarily Japanese tourists was identified by Dr. Hiroaki Ota, a Japanese psychiatrist who was working in Paris in the early 1980s. His thesis, while initially accepted by the psychiatric profession, crumbled when I revealed to them that identity is a narrative and that Ota just thought he was a Japanese psychiatrist studying Japanese tourists, Japanese tourists who came to believe that they didn't exist and that Paris didn't exist, even though they were walking around Paris speaking Japanese. The psychiatric profession was horrified to find out that Hiroaki Ota was actually Dr. Youcef Mahmoudia, and that Mahmoudia had already demonstrated that so-called Paris Syndrome was actually just a form of jet lag, culture shock and over excitement about being in a famous but unknown city, which caused the pulse rate to become quite rapid and create mental disorientation. (Editor's note: I write from Paris, where I fear that my life may be in danger, my anxiety is growing by the hour, and while I can no longer substantiate my own existence, I can say that the Parisian night life is just plain unreal. Nosirrah may be on to something here. Nosirrah's theory that Ota and his nemesis Mahmoudia are actually one and the same person seems to be unsupported by any evidence, however there is an absence of any trace of Hiroaki Ota in Paris and no evidence that he exists at all, except that the Japanese Embassy has claimed to this editor that Ota does exist but will not provide any supporting proof, and further, the Japanese Embassy in Paris maintains a Paris Syndrome hotline for its visiting citizens who fall prey to the imaginary Paris Syndrome discovered by an imaginary Dr. Hiroaki Ota. Is the Japanese Embassy too embarrassed to admit that their hotline is for a non-existent malady, or is this part of a wider cover up? Meanwhile, Mahmoudia is most definitely listed at the oldest hospital in Paris, the Hôtel-Dieu de Paris, although we could obtain no further response from that hospital when we asked them to address the allegations that Mahmoudia and Ota were in fact the same and that there is a demand from the public that the existence of at least one of them be verified. We will invite our readers to research this mystery further as the resources of a small publishing house are not up to penetrating what may be an unparalleled government conspiracy, and I don't know if they will try to stop me from getting these words out to the world. My heart is racing, I know not what to do except to try to get out of Paris. I have heard that Florence is beautiful this time of year.)

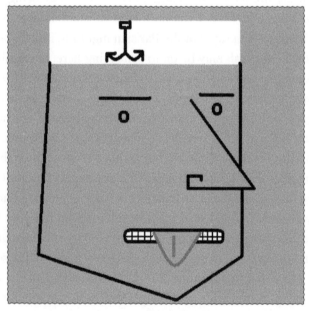

Dr. Youcef Mahmoudia

This is Nosirrah again, and yes it was Hôtel-Dieu de Paris where I was successfully treated for Japanese Tourist Identity by a man claiming to be Dr. Mahmoudia, but whom I could tell was actually Dr. Ota. I was treated very effectively by being placed in front of a mirror, where it became obvious that I was not Japanese and so I was released. But that isn't what is important. What is important is that when I discovered that I was in Paris and not in Jerusalem, I was standing at 27 rue de Fleurus. Somehow I had found my way home.

I will not repeat here the story of my childhood, other than to quote from my tour de force novella *God Is an Atheist:*

> I actually have no memory of childhood, but with the help of a skilled and compassionate therapist, I reconstructed those early years. Consider my writing and you will understand that its origins are deeper than the experiences of this one body-mind, and perhaps that will compel you to accept what I have to tell you. Franz Kafka impregnated Alice B. Toklas in a chance encounter in Berlin in 1923 after a night of heavy drinking and cannabis smoking, and, I, Nosirrah, am the result of that undocumented tryst. This weird occurrence, when Toklas was 46 and just a year before Kafka died of self-starvation, was never revealed to Gertrude Stein, who thought Toklas was just eating too many brownies. This resulted in a childhood where Nosirrah was literally and figuratively hidden in plain sight in the Paris apartment, never spoken of, never spoken to, and may have resulted in the deep

questioning of his very existence. I am Nosirrah, I am that child, now old, but not as old as it would seem doing the math, for I have also found some secrets of staying young.

One of those secrets, which I will share with you, is do not under any circumstances believe in the story of your life, do not believe the confirmations of a compassionate therapist as she helps you rebuild your past. As the stories are told and confirmed, over and over, you will come to remember them as if they actually occurred. Nothing occurs. Everything is story, everything is constructed. The past only exists as you build it, and its burden is only the one that you take on by your own creation.

So you have my autobiography, you have the fragmented memories of my childhood, the inspiring stories of a father and a husband, the wanderings of a seeker, the enlightenment at the feet of the masters, and you have gotten an unusual bonus, which is to say, my account of my death. Most autobiographies do not include a description of the author's death and that is an unfortunate oversight, possibly because the writer typically has either ended the story of his own life at a point prior to death or in dying he has stopped describing his life.

My having died at a young age gives this tome an unusual added value, and I hope that you will consider this before you attempt to return this book for full credit.

I have, of course, considered a second death, one in which my body does not take in my consciousness, rejecting it for a final time and leaving me therefore in the endless field of consciousness without the gravitational pull of the body appetites. You may wonder what this consciousness might be like without any attraction to the breath, with no desire for the human touch and no hunger for a poached asparagus compote on a bed of locally sourced, organic arugula with a side of steamed Peruvian quinoa, topped with a Balsamic vinaigrette drizzle, all paired with an appropriate Napa Valley merlot or perhaps one of the local micro-brewery IPAs. This meal, with a beautiful companion across the table (who hopefully will pick up the tab), eyes focused on mine, telling me that yes, I am alive, I am loved, I am the center of the whole Universe. Now we take each other's hands as we go up to the LEEDs certified room with organic cotton sheets and memory foam mattress, where we encounter each other on the tantric plane, beyond pleasure, beyond self, heart bursting with the Full Energy of Life and the slight blockage from years of failure to even so much as walk around the block for exercise, that slight blockage becoming the Hoover Dam with all the frisky frolicking in the Organic Tantra, and blam...dead. That is a conscious death and totally sustainable. This is the story of my second death, one that is yet to come but will be as told here. My spiritual path is to practice this night after night, relentlessly, with all whom I meet, until the one who bursts my heart appears.

I would be remiss in recounting my life and my death without including the lessons learned in such a life, lessons which may be of use to those who read this book looking for guidance.

My editor has insisted on this section, as she believes that while this book is certainly unsellable, there is the possibility of coffee mugs with pithy quotes, t-shirts with catchy phrases, bumper stickers with funny sayings, and a calendar with pictures of cute cats with excerpts from the book just because cats sell and excerpts from this book don't.

So, here is some of my guidance for you:

APHORISMS SELL MUGS BUT DON'T TRANSFORM PEOPLE

My name is Trudy and I am a crazy calico.
I love to chase yarn balls around the room.
(That's for the cat calendar.)

**Life is a bowl of cherries
and then you die**

I SAW GOD AND ALL I GOT WAS THIS LOUSY T-SHIRT

Help, I'm having an in-the-body experience

MY SPIRITUAL TEACHER CAN BEAT UP
YOUR HONOR STUDENT

**IF YOU CAN
READ THIS
COFFEE MUG,
YOU'RE DRIVING
TOO CLOSE**

Don't honk if you meditate

I have compromised myself enough now. That should be enough to get you through your life and also fund the deficit caused by the publication of this book. Many great artists had to prostitute themselves to continue their art, and I am no exception. For the purists among you, please forgive me the prior commercial break. My true guidance is simple: You don't need a guide, so don't ask for guidance. Spend your life with what you don't know, what you know will always be waiting. Confusion is your friend, hang out together as much as possible. Emptiness doesn't need to be filled by action, it is filled by life.

I must wrap up this biographical narrative with a picture of where life is today. All that I have seen, all that I have achieved, all that I have become amounts to the dust on my desk as I write this. All that you will ever accumulate in your life, all the honors and all the failures, all the wounds and all the love, all of this in its totality is dust. This is not a pejorative, it is an invitation to release yourself from the burden of your collecting of memories and experiences. Imagine a life that is freed from the past, open and available to the nuances of full contact with the world.

Creativity is not your production of things. It is the embrace of emptiness, the letting go of all that is known, the plunge into nothingness. There at the border between something and nothing, you will feel the push-back from the universe itself. This movement, the resistance to nothingness, is the creative and animating energy that flows through each of us. This requires the sacrifice of your ideas and constructs. From this void of unknowing thrust the forms of what is new. You won't know it until you see it. Once you see it, you will know it. What you know is not it. What you know must be thrown into the fire so that what is new can emerge once more, and again you will know it when you see it, and again you will have to discard what you know to get to what is new, to what is next.

From this you can live, you can work, you can love, you can raise your family, you can write or paint, sing or dance. This energy of creation will continue to form the language, the expression, the culture that we all reside in. The culture of the past decays as the next culture arises. The mind that knows it does not know is always ready for what is next, while what is old resides as echo, but not actual. We can utilize the old because we know what it is, we don't see it as current, and in that contact with the actual we can extract utility from the past without deluding ourselves that it is still alive.

Find each other, those who live in the present and ride the wave of what is next, it is time to co-create, to collaborate, to move in harmonic connection and live what is perceived. The societal forms are breaking down and this open space waits for the creative. You are that, nothing less than the movement of the universe creating something out of nothing, and nothing out of something. This is the story of my life, it is the story of your life, and it is, in the end, the autobiography of life itself.

Sentient Publications, LLC publishes nonfiction books on cultural creativity, experimental education, transformative spirituality, holistic health, new science, ecology, and other topics, approached from an integral viewpoint. We also publish fiction that aims to intrigue, stimulate, and entertain. Our authors are intensely interested in exploring the nature of life from fresh perspectives, addressing life's great questions, and fostering the full expression of the human potential. Sentient Publications' books arise from the spirit of inquiry and the richness of the inherent dialogue between writer and reader.

Our Culture Tools series is designed to give social catalyzers and cultural entrepreneurs the essential information, technology, and inspiration to forge a sustainable, creative, and compassionate world.

We are very interested in hearing from our readers. To direct suggestions or comments to us, or to be added to our mailing list, please contact:

SENTIENT PUBLICATIONS, LLC
1113 Spruce Street
Boulder, CO 80302
303-443-2188
contact@sentientpublications.com
www.sentientpublications.com